Acting Edition

Rodgers & |

Sta

Music by
Richard Rodgers

Lyrics by
Oscar Hammerstein II

Book by
Tom Briggs & Louis Mattioli

Based on the screenplay by Oscar Hammerstein II
and the novel by Phil Stong

CONCORD
THEATRICALS

ISBN 978-0-573-70930-2

www.concordtheatricals.com
www.concordtheatricals.co.uk

FOR PRODUCTION INQUIRIES

UNITED STATES AND CANADA
info@concordtheatricals.com
1-866-979-0447

UNITED KINGDOM AND EUROPE
licensing@concordtheatricals.co.uk
020-7054-7298

Each title is subject to availability from Concord Theatricals Corp., depending upon country of performance. Please be aware that *STATE FAIR* may not be licensed by Concord Theatricals Corp. in your territory. Professional and amateur producers should contact the nearest Concord Theatricals Corp. office or licensing partner to verify availability.

This work is published by R&H Theatricals, an imprint of Concord Theatricals Corp.

STATE FAIR opened on Broadway at the Music Box Theatre on March 27, 1996. (David Merrick presents the Theatre Guild production. Thomas Viertel, Executive Producer. Produced by Robert Franz, Philip Langner, Natalie Lloyd, Jonathan C. Herzog, Meredith Blair, and Gordon Smith in association with Mark N. Sirangelo and the PGI Entertainment Company. Pre-Broadway National Tour produced by Sonny Everett, Bonnie Nelson Schwartz, Matt Garfield, and Ron Kumin. Associate Producers David Young and Norma Langworthy. By arrangement with Celia Lipton Productions, Inc. In association with the North Carolina School of the Arts Foundation.) The production was directed by James Hammerstein and Randy Skinner, with scenic design by James Leonard Joy, costume design by Michael Bottari and Ronald Case, lighting design by Natasha Katz, sound design by Brian Ronan, musical direction and vocal arrangements by Kay Cameron, orchestrations by Bruce Pomahac, dance arrangements by Scot Woolley, music coordination by John Miller, hair design by George M. Fraggos, technical supervision by Gene O'Donovan, and casting by Caro Jones, C.S.A. and Pat McCorkle, C.S.A. The production stage manager was Warren Crane, the general manager was Ralph Roseman, the general press representative was Susan L. Schulman, and the choreographer was Randy Skinner. The cast was as follows:

ABEL FRAKE	John Davidson
GUS	James Patterson
MARGY FRAKE	Andrea McArdle
MELISSA FRAKE	Kathryn Crosby
WAYNE FRAKE	Ben Wright
DAVE MILLER	Charles Goff
ELEANOR	Susan Haefner
HARRY	Peter Benson
THE FAIR ANNOUNCER	J. Lee Flynn
THE HOOP-LA BARKER	Tim Fauvel
EMILY ARDEN	Donna McKechnie
THE ASTOUNDING STRALENKO	Steve Steiner
VIVIAN	Tina Johnson
JEANNE	Leslie Bell
PAT GILBERT	Scott Wise
CHARLIE	Darrian C. Ford
LEM	John Wilkerson
CLAY	J. Lee Flynn
HANK MUNSON	Newton R. Gilchrist
THE CHIEF OF POLICE	Steve Steiner

VIOLET .... Jackie Angelescu

THE FAIRTONES .... Ian Knauer, James Patterson,
Michael Lee Scott, Scott Willis

JUDGE HEPPENSTAHL .... Charles Goff

MRS. EDWIN METCALF OF POTTSVILLE ...... Jacquiline Rohrbacker

2 ROUSTABOUTS .... Scott Willis, Michael Lee Scott

BARKERS, VENDORS, JUDGES, FAIRGOERS ....Kelli Barclay,
Leslie Bell, Linnea Dakin, SuEllen Estey, Tim Fauvel,
Amy Gage, Susan Haefner, Tina Johnson, Ian Knauer,
Julie Lira, James Patterson, John Scott, Michael Lee Scott,
Mary C. Sheehan, Steve Steiner, Scott Willis

CHARACTERS

(in order of appearance)

ABEL FRAKE – a farmer

GUS – the Frakes' hired man

MARGY FRAKE – the Frakes' daughter

MELISSA FRAKE – Abel's wife

WAYNE FRAKE – the Frakes' son

DAVE MILLER – the local storekeeper

ELEANOR – Wayne's girlfriend

HARRY – Margy's boyfriend

THE FAIR ANNOUNCER

THE HOOP-LA BARKER

EMILY ARDEN

THE ASTOUNDING STRALENKO

VIVIAN – a cooch dancer

JEANNE – a cooch dancer

PAT GILBERT – a newspaper reporter

CHARLIE – a newspaper photographer

LEM – a farmer

CLAY – a farmer

HANK MUNSON – a farmer

THE CHIEF OF POLICE

VIOLET – his daughter

THE FAIRTONES

JUDGE HEPPENSTAHL

MRS. EDWIN METCALF OF POTTSVIILE

2 ROUSTABOUTS

BARKERS, VENDORS, JUDGES, FAIRGOERS

SETTING

The action takes place over five days in late August of 1946 on the Frake farm in Brunswick, Iowa and at the Iowa State Fair in Des Moines.

INCLUSION STATEMENT

In this show, the race of the characters is not pivotal to the plot. We encourage you to consider diversity and inclusion in your casting choices.

AUTHOR'S NOTE

State Fair is a story that has been told for over sixty years. Phil Stong's novel was published in 1932, and its first motion picture version was released the following year. Rodgers and Hammerstein musicalized the story for the 1945 movie, and an updated remake was released in 1962. So this stage version is the next incarnation of *State Fair*, and while modern tastes and mores have changed with the times, this story's appeal has never waned. I think that's because *State Fair* is an honest story of an American heartland tradition, the essence of which has remained virtually unchanged during the past century. Some might consider aspects of this musical to be corny, but for a show set in Iowa, I take that as a compliment. Once, when Oscar Hammerstein II was accused of being corny, he freely admitted to it. "But isn't life sometimes corny?" he asked, and of course it is. What could be cornier than a tentative young couple in the moonlight sharing a first kiss? Or an animal so beloved he's like a member of the family? But such things do happen, they are real, and *State Fair* must be played for real (especially when it gets a little corny). Only if the audience believes in the reality of each character's story will they jump aboard the emotional roller coaster the characters ride throughout the show and follow their stories with relish.

Abel and Melissa truly enjoy each other and have a playful, time-tested relationship. They are vital farm folk who are not reticent about being affectionate with each other. If Melissa is a bit of a worrywart and tends to be a little high-strung, it's because she cares so much about her family's well-being. And although Abel may seem gruff and preoccupied at times, he's a big-hearted man who never fails to come through with the emotional support his wife and kids have come to rely upon.

Margy is discovering what she doesn't want and is on the verge of doing something about it. It's what she *does* want that confuses her. Typical of a Hammerstein heroine, she's strong and bright but not worldly, and she knows when the right guy has come along.

Pat is a newspaperman whose combat experience, both in WWII and with women, has made him a cynic. But like Margy, he is on the brink of change. When he first approaches Margy on the midway, he should suggest the danger inherent in a girl getting swept off her feet by a far more experienced man. He is hung up on past glories and disappointments, while Margy is looking to the future. It's her fervent point of view that inspires in Pat the self-confidence and esteem he needs to start looking forward.

Harry's marriage proposal to Margy must be a viable possibility for her. Although Harry is clearly a comic character, it's important that the audience not experience him merely as a buffoon, and that they believe Margy might end up with him. He's earnest, enthusiastic, practical, and utterly devoted to Margy – not bad qualities in a fella, or a husband.

Wayne is actually more naive than his younger sister. He's inexperienced and insecure, although he thinks he has his life all figured out. When a sophisticated knock-out like Emily Arden appears out of nowhere and befriends him, his world is suddenly turned upside down. You shouldn't blame him if his emotions and his hormones run wild. But in his heart, he's still an innocent with a genuine quality that Emily recognizes and tries to protect. He really belongs back at home with his girlfriend, Eleanor.

Emily is not a villain. In a story about a naive young man and the worldly woman who breaks his heart, it's easy to blame her for everything. So it's important that the audience focus on the moment in Act I, Scene Seven when Emily sets guidelines for Wayne concerning their relationship, and again when she reiterates them in Act I, Scene Ten, when he pushes. Although there have probably been many Waynes in her life, she is no less hurt than Wayne when they eventually part. And do keep in mind that both she and Wayne are, after all, adults.

The ensemble is a big asset to any production and should be full of individual and distinct personalities. In fact, they *are* the fair, bringing great character background to the midway scenes even when they are not being featured. And there should be kids in the show – the more, the merrier. They bring lots of life to the stage and help reinforce the familial environment that is the heart of the play.

The $5 bet between Abel and Dave Miller, which bookends the story, is important to the arc of the show. Miller's cynicism provides contrast to the sentimentality in the rest of the story. You can make sure the audience keeps that bet in mind by having Abel keep it in mind. He mentions the bet in Act I, Scene Nine, after Melissa wins her competition, and when he is disappointed by his hog, Blue Boy, at the top of Act II, he fears losing the bet as much as he fears his hog losing the competition. In Act II, Scene Five, Abel is on top of the world until the heartbroken Wayne stumbles on and, again, the bet looks to be in jeopardy. In the last scene, the bet ultimately hinges on Margy's answer to Miller as to whether or not she had a good time at the fair, and Abel's tension awaiting her answer should be palpable. These moments will really pay off when, at the final curtain, Abel puts out his hand to Miller for the $5 and the audience is as delighted by his triumph as Abel himself.

Now a word about the pig. It is inevitable that someone will come up with the notion of using a live hog. Don't. I have always believed that the audience does a much better job of conjuring up their own image of this magnificent beast than could ever be shown them. And more importantly, if Blue Boy is introduced as an onstage character, his story should be dramatized, or the audience will feel cheated. But smart as they are, believe me, boars do not "perform" – they are uncontrollable onstage (in more ways than one). Blue Boy's impact on the story has only to do with his effect on Abel, from the bet with Miller through the pride of "More Than Just A Friend," the rage and disappointment at the top of Act II, and the subsequent euphoria of victory. It's all about Abel, not the hog.

Although there are a large number of scenes, don't let that scare you. Each location can be perfectly suggested with just a piece or two of well-chosen scenery and props. What's most important is that the play move fluidly from one scene to another. No single piece of scenery is worth delaying the storytelling or slowing the pace. This is an easy story to follow, so it has to keep moving or the audience will get ahead of it. It's probably a good idea to figure out the midway scenes first, as colorful and entertaining as possible, because you'll be spending a lot of time there.

And, hey – have a great time at the fair!

Tom Briggs
July 1997
New York City

MUSICAL NUMBERS

ACT I

"Our State Fair" . . . . .Abel, Melissa, Wayne

"It Might As Well Be Spring". . . . . .Margy

"Driving At Night". . . . . .The Frakes

"Our State Fair (Reprise)". . . . . .Ensemble

"That's For Me". . . . . .Wayne

"More Than Just A Friend" . . . . Abel, Lem, Clay, Hank

"Isn't It Kinda Fun?" . . . . Pat & Margy

"You Never Had It So Good" . . . . Emily Arden & The Fairtones

"It Might As Well Be Spring (Reprise)" . . . . .Margy

"When I Go Out Walking With My Baby". . . . . Abel & Melissa

"So Far" . . . . .Wayne & Emily

"It's A Grand Night For Singing". . . . . Company

ACT II

"The Man I Used To Be". . . . . Pat, Vivian, Jeanne

"All I Owe Ioway". . . . . Abel & Company

"The Man I Used To Be (Reprise)" . . . . .Pat

"Isn't It Kinda Fun? (Reprise)" . . . . .Margy

"That's The Way It Happens". . . . . Emily Arden & The Fairtones

"Boys And Girls Like You And Me". Abel & Melissa

"The Next Time It Happens" . . . . .Margy

ACT I

[MUSIC NO. 01 "OVERTURE"]

Scene One
The Frake Farm
A Tuesday Afternoon in Late August 1946

[MUSIC NO. 02 "OUR STATE FAIR"]

(To one side of the stage is the kitchen corner at the back of a warm, old, two-story farmhouse. A screen door leads out onto the porch and into the yard, an archway leading off into the rest of the house. A juneberry tree shades a barn upstage in the distance. Split-rail fencing extends offstage to both sides, holding back overgrown foliage, and the yard is strewn with the many provisions associated with a camping trip. Upstage is a livestock trailer and an old Ford pickup truck. The trailer ornately proclaims: "Blue Boy – Abel Frake, Brunswick: Owner." Thereon is painted a depiction of what surely must be the most magnificent Hampshire boar in captivity.)

*(***MELISSA FRAKE*** is in the kitchen preparing a crock of mincemeat; ***WAYNE FRAKE*** and ***GUS***, the Frakes' hired man, are upstage hitching Blue Boy's trailer to the truck; ***ABEL FRAKE*** is dumping a bucket of garbage into a large barrel and stirring it with a long stick.)*

ABEL.

> OUR STATE FAIR IS A GREAT STATE FAIR –
> DON'T MISS IT, DON'T EVEN BE LATE.
> IT'S DOLLARS TO DOUGHNUTS THAT OUR STATE FAIR
> IS THE BEST STATE FAIR IN OUR STATE!

> *(The music continues.)*

Gimme a hand, Gus. Blue Boy'll want a little snack, ya know how uppity he gets when he has to travel.

> *(**ABEL** and **GUS** take the barrel off upstage, almost running down **MARGY FRAKE** as she enters, absorbed in a magazine.)*

Look out, Margy!

MARGY. Sorry.

> *(**ABEL** and **GUS** exit; **MARGY** sits on the fence, continuing to read her magazine.)*

MELISSA.

> OUR STATE FAIR IS A GREAT STATE FAIR –
> DON'T MISS IT, DON'T EVEN BE LATE.
> IT'S DOLLARS TO DOUGHNUTS THAT OUR STATE FAIR
> IS THE BEST STATE FAIR IN OUR STATE!

> *(The music continues as she calls off upstairs:)*

Margy, come gimme a hand with these pickles.

> *(**MARGY**, engrossed in her magazine, doesn't respond.)*

Margy? Oh, where is that girl?

> *(**MELISSA** exits through the archway as **WAYNE** crosses, carrying several embroidery hoops.)*

WAYNE. *(To* **MARGY.***)* Hey, Sis, do ya mind? I'm tryin' to practice here.

MARGY. Sorry.

> *(She exits.)*

WAYNE.

OUR STATE FAIR IS A GREAT STATE FAIR –
DON'T MISS IT, DON'T EVEN BE LATE.
IT'S DOLLARS TO DOUGHNUTS THAT OUR STATE FAIR
IS THE BEST STATE FAIR IN OUR STATE!

> *(The music continues.)*

Okay, mister – now I'll try for that pearl necklace in the back row.

> *(He tosses a hoop and rings a fence post.)*

"Ding!" Hand over the pearls, mister.

(Pretending to hand the necklace to someone.) That's for you, Eleanor. And now I'll take a shot at that pocket watch over there.

> *(He tosses another hoop over the post.)*

"Ding!" That's for me!

> *(***WAYNE*** continues practicing as* ***ABEL*** *and* ***GUS*** *enter upstage.)*

ABEL. Now make him a nice soft bed, Gus. Ya know how Blue Boy feels about potholes and I can't be expected to miss 'em all.

> *(***GUS*** *grabs a pitchfork and starts pitching hay into the back of the trailer;* ***ABEL*** *turns his attention to a length of rope, winding it up around his elbow and shoulder.)*

OUR STATE FAIR IS A...

(**MELISSA** *enters in the kitchen and resumes preparing her mincemeat.*)

MELISSA.
OUR STATE FAIR IS A...

WAYNE.
OUR STATE FAIR IS A...

(**ABEL, MELISSA,** *and* **WAYNE** *sing in a round:*)

ABEL, MELISSA & WAYNE.
...GREAT STATE FAIR –
DON'T MISS IT, DON'T EVEN BE LATE.
IT'S DOLLARS TO DOUGHNUTS THAT OUR STATE FAIR
IS THE BEST STATE FAIR...

(*They are interrupted by the distinctive horn of an old jalopy pulling up offstage, and* **GUS** *exits. Music continues.*)

ABEL. Well, it's high time Dave Miller got here with that special feed. He knows how peckish Blue Boy gets when he's under pressure.

(**MELISSA** *exits through the archway as* **DAVE MILLER** *enters;* **GUS** *follows him on, a large sack of feed balanced precariously on his shoulder. It looks to be easily fifty pounds and is marked "G.H. Brand." Music out.*)

MILLER. Afternoon, Abel, Wayne.

ABEL. We'd just about given up hope o' seein' ya, Dave.

(*He crosses to* **GUS** *and inspects the feed, sniffing and tapping the sack.*)

WAYNE. Why ya got on your galoshes, Mr. Miller? Are they predicting bad weather?

MILLER. Nope. They're predicting good weather. That's why I got on my galoshes.

*(**WAYNE** exits as **GUS** crosses upstage, loads the bag into the back of the truck, then goes off for another as **WAYNE** enters to the truck with a bag the same size. This continues, **WAYNE** and **GUS** crossing back and forth to the truck with bags of feed, throughout the scene.)*

ABEL. I tell ya, Dave, Blue Boy's gonna win the Grand Sweepstakes so easy, they'll ask J. Edgar Hoover to look into it.

MILLER. I wouldn't count on it, Abel.

ABEL. Why not? He's the finest boar in the state.

MILLER. Well if that's true, he's as good as beat.

ABEL. Whaddaya talkin' about?

MILLER. Abel, if man or hog ever got what he was entitled to – just once – the eternal stars would quit makin' melody in their spheres and all that.

ABEL. Poppycock! I say Blue Boy's the best and so will the judges.

MILLER. They might, only then something might go wrong for Wayne or Margy. Mark my words, Abel – there's a law of compensation in this world. For every good there's a bad. Now Ralph Waldo Emerson tells us...

ABEL. I don't care what Waldo Emerson says! I got five dollars says we go to the fair and Blue Boy wins the sweepstakes and nothin' bad happens to him or me or my family.

MILLER. If you'd asked me, I'd have given ya ten to one. But ya didn't, so it's an even bet – five dollars.

ABEL. *(They shake on it.)* Five dollars is right!

*(**GUS** and **WAYNE** have loaded the last of the feed into the truck. **GUS** exits, and **WAYNE** crosses downstage.)*

MILLER. I'll be around on Saturday after supper for the money.

ABEL. Be around *with* the money, ya mean.

MILLER. Ha! That'd be a first!

(He exits.)

ABEL. Old grump. He could look at a bed of roses and see ragweed. Waldo Emerson...!

(He exits upstage, and **WAYNE** *resumes practicing with the hoops.* **MELISSA** *enters in the kitchen and crosses out onto the porch.)*

MELISSA. Wayne, where's Margy?

WAYNE. I dunno. She's around here somewhere.

MELISSA. *(Exasperated.)* Well, I know that.

(She exits around the side of the house.)

WAYNE. Okay, mister – now I'll try for that fake revolver with the genuine simulated pearl handle.

ELEANOR. *(Offstage.)* Wayne! ...Wayne!

WAYNE. Back here, Eleanor.

*(***ELEANOR** *comes running on.)*

ELEANOR. Oh, Wayne, I have the most wonderful news...

(She throws herself into his arms, and he spins her around.)

WAYNE. Well now, slow down and tell me...

ELEANOR. *(Holding up an envelope.)* From State College. Somebody dropped out of the nursing program and I got accepted. I'm going off to college in ten days!

WAYNE. Well, gee...that's...

(The gravity of the situation suddenly strikes him.)

Ten days?

ELEANOR. Of course now I can't go to the fair.

WAYNE. Whaddaya talkin' about? I got the three days all planned out for us.

ELEANOR. Honeybunch, I got a million and one things on my mind.

WAYNE. Can't one of 'em be me? I suppose when ya get home next summer you'll be educated to the point where I'll look pretty ignorant and ya won't find me very interesting anymore.

ELEANOR. Oh, Wayne – there'll never be anybody like you.

WAYNE. It's not somebody like me I'm worried about. It's somebody different – some guy with a blazer and a trust fund.

ELEANOR. And just exactly what is that supposed to mean? It sounds like you think I'm not to be trusted.

WAYNE. Well, how am I supposed to know what's goin' on? Between the sorority house and the freshman mixer, traipsin' around with Lord knows who.

ELEANOR. *(Seething.)* I do not traipse!

WAYNE. Or whatever you Gamma Hubba-Hubba girls call it.

ELEANOR. Well, Mr. Frake, I never realized you held me in such low regard. *(She storms away across the yard.)*

WAYNE. Now hold on, Eleanor –

ELEANOR. *(Turning back to him.)* I should have known better than to think you'd be happy for me.

(She exits upstage. **WAYNE** *turns to exit and nearly runs into* **MARGY**, *who has entered and heard the last of their argument.)*

WAYNE. Women.

(He exits. **MARGY** *wanders across the yard, tearing the petals from a daisy one by one.* **MELISSA** *enters in the kitchen and sees* **MARGY** *in the yard.)*

MELISSA. *(Calling out the screen door.)* Oh, Margy – there you are. Come help me label these pickles.

MARGY. *(To herself, disdainfully.)* Pickles.

(She throws down the flower and crosses through the screen door into the kitchen.)

MELISSA. Have you finished your packing?

MARGY. Pretty near.

MELISSA. How close is that to done?

MARGY. Pretty near.

(Picking up a label and a pen.) Do you want your name "Mrs. Abel Frake" or "Mrs. Melissa Frake"?

MELISSA. Oh... Melissa, I guess. What with your father entering Blue Boy, I'd hate for the judges to get us mixed up.

MARGY. I've never seen Daddy so hepped up as he is about Blue Boy winning the sweepstakes.

MELISSA. Sweepstakes, my foot. He won't really be happy until that pig makes "Who's Who."

*(**MARGY** accidentally knocks a pan off the counter, clanging to the floor.)*

Oh, Margy...

MARGY. I'm sorry, I'm sorry, a thousand times sorry!

MELISSA. Doesn't know what she's doin' one minute to the next.

MARGY. Pickles and pigs, pigs and pickles... Who cares about the stupid old state fair anyway?

MELISSA. Why, Margaret Elizabeth Frake – you've always loved the fair. What's gotten into you lately, anyhow? All you do is sit around and mope.

MARGY. *(Moping.)* I don't sit around and mope.

MELISSA. Why don't you take those jars out and wrap 'em up for me.

> **[MUSIC NO. 03 "IT MIGHT AS WELL BE SPRING"]**
>
> (**MARGY** *takes the crate of jars out onto the porch as* **MELISSA** *exits.*)

MARGY. "I don't know what's gotten into you lately."

> *(She sits on the steps of the porch, wrapping each jar in a cloth napkin before packing it in the crate; she pauses.)*

What *has* gotten into me anyway?

THE THINGS I USED TO LIKE
I DON'T LIKE ANYMORE.
I WANT A LOT OF OTHER THINGS
I'VE NEVER HAD BEFORE.
IT'S JUST LIKE MOTHER SAYS –
I SIT AROUND AND MOPE,
PRETENDING I AM WONDERFUL
AND KNOWING I'M A DOPE!

I'M AS RESTLESS AS A WILLOW IN A WINDSTORM,
I'M AS JUMPY AS A PUPPET ON A STRING.
I'D SAY THAT I HAD SPRING FEVER,
BUT I KNOW IT ISN'T SPRING.
I AM STARRY-EYED AND VAGUELY DISCONTENTED,

MARGY.

LIKE A NIGHTINGALE WITHOUT A SONG TO SING.
OH, WHY SHOULD I HAVE SPRING FEVER
WHEN IT ISN'T EVEN SPRING?

I KEEP WISHING I WERE SOMEWHERE ELSE,
WALKING DOWN A STRANGE NEW STREET,
HEARING WORDS THAT I HAVE NEVER HEARD
FROM A MAN I'VE YET TO MEET.

I'M AS BUSY AS A SPIDER SPINNING DAYDREAMS,
I'M AS GIDDY AS A BABY ON A SWING.
I HAVEN'T SEEN A CROCUS OR A ROSEBUD
OR A ROBIN ON THE WING,
BUT I FEEL SO GAY – IN A MELANCHOLY WAY –
THAT IT MIGHT AS WELL BE SPRING...
IT MIGHT AS WELL BE SPRING.

> *(**MELISSA** enters in the kitchen and again turns her attention to the mincemeat. **ABEL** enters in the yard upstage; **MELISSA** takes a spoonful of mincemeat and crosses out onto the porch.)*

MELISSA. Abel, come here. I want your opinion.

> *(**ABEL** sniffs the mincemeat then tastes it, elaborately shifting it in his mouth before swallowing.)*

ABEL. Don't taste like Gram's. It's flat.

MELISSA. I followed her recipe.

ABEL. No, Mother, ya left somethin' out.

MELISSA. Abel Frake, I will not put liquor in my cooking.

> *(She grabs the spoon from **ABEL** and goes back into the kitchen.)*

ABEL. *(Following her.)* Can't make mincemeat without brandy. Ain't no such thing.

MELISSA. I don't approve of it and I won't do it!

ABEL. Well, you'll be sorry. Ya know, those judges at the fair like to take a little nip now and again.

MELISSA. What you do in the privacy of our home is your business, but I will not broadcast the drunken habits of this family all over the state! Now get those suitcases from the front hall.

ABEL. I'm on my way, Mother.

> *(He exits through the archway.* **MELISSA** *takes a deep breath, crosses to the cupboard, and takes out a quart bottle of brandy. She removes the cap, but then reconsiders.)*

MELISSA. No, I won't do it.

> *(She replaces the cap and hurries the bottle back to the cupboard. She crosses out the screen door and exits around the side of the house as* **ABEL** *enters in the kitchen with the suitcases. He sees the crock and stops; he looks out the screen door to make certain he's unobserved, then slips over to the cupboard and takes out the brandy. He pours a good slug into the crock, gives it a stir, scoops out a bit with his finger, and tastes it.)*

ABEL. Aw, what the hell – ya can't fly on one wing.

> *(He pours several "glugs" into the crock, gives it a stir, and takes another taste; smacking his lips.)*

Now that's the ticket!

(He returns the bottle to the cupboard, takes the suitcases, crosses out the screen door and across the yard to the truck as **HARRY** *enters.)*

ABEL. Hiya, Harry, whaddaya know?

HARRY. Not much.

ABEL. Yep.

*(***ABEL*** *exits.* **HARRY** *sneaks up behind* **MARGY** *and covers her eyes.)*

HARRY. Guess who.

MARGY. Hi, Harry.

HARRY. *(Enticingly.)* I saw something this morning.

MARGY. What?

HARRY. Sweetest bit of farmland this side of Davenport. I was thinkin' of puttin' in a bid. That is, if you like it.

MARGY. Has it got a house on it?

HARRY. Yeah, but it's too old. We'll have to level it and build a new one.

MARGY. Why? I like old houses.

HARRY. Won't go with our modern kind of farm. Scientific irrigation, electric milking machines and get this – individual hen roosts, separate and sanitary, like...like a chicken maternity ward! Nope, no old clapboard and shingle type house for us. There's a new kinda plastic, pre-fabricated job.

MARGY. Is it pretty?

HARRY. Sure! Wait'll ya see the catalogue – they even tell ya how to furnish it. No carpets or rugs – they're just dust collectors.

MARGY. What's on the floors?

HARRY. *(Importantly.)* Linoleum.

MARGY. Throughout the whole house?

HARRY. It's slick and smooth and easy to keep clean – like...like every room in the house was a bathroom.

MARGY. Sounds real cozy.

HARRY. Sure! Only way to live – everything sanitary.

> (**MELISSA** *enters upstage with a wash basin, crosses into the kitchen, and exits through the archway.*)

Sure wish I was goin' to the fair with ya, only I can't neglect Daisy just when she's about to calve.

MARGY. I understand, Harry. I know the farm comes first.

HARRY. Ya know, I've been thinkin' – after our wedding...

MARGY. *(Crossing away.)* Now Harry...

HARRY. I know, I know – it's not for sure yet. But I've been thinkin' – maybe we'd take a trip somewhere.

MARGY. You mean a honeymoon.

HARRY. *(Moving to her.)* That's what! And somewhere nice, too, like maybe Chicago. See the Museum of Science and Industry, take the el to the stockyards.

> (**MARGY** *doesn't react.*)

'Course one night you'd probably get all slickered up and we'd paint the town – maybe go dancing.

MARGY. Sounds like a wonderful trip, Harry.

HARRY. Then can I take that as a yes?

> (**WAYNE** *and* **GUS** *enter upstage carrying guide paddles, interrupting the romantic mood* **HARRY** *is trying to set. They call out, "Hey, Harry," as they cross and exit.*)

HARRY. C'mon, Margy, whaddaya say? You know I haven't made a plan since I was twelve that didn't include you.

MARGY. I...I can't say anything right now, Harry.

HARRY. After the fair, then?

MARGY. Maybe.

HARRY. *(Breaking away from her.)* "Maybe." It's always "maybe" with you. How long ya gonna keep me waitin', Marge? After all, we've graduated high school now – it's time to get on with our lives.

MARGY. *(Taking a deep breath.)* Okay, Harry. I'll give you an answer after the fair.

HARRY. You mean it, Margy?

MARGY. Promise.

HARRY. Oh, that's swell!

> *(He moves to kiss her but is distracted by a roaring squeal from offstage.)*

[MUSIC NO. 03A "BLUE BOY ENTERS"]

Wow!

> *(**HARRY** races upstage as **ABEL** enters and swings open the door at the back of Blue Boy's trailer. The door opens downstage, blocking our view as **GUS** and **WAYNE** usher Blue Boy into the trailer. A cloud of dust rises from behind a row of foliage to a symphony of squeals and grunts; the trailer begins rocking violently. **GUS** closes the door at the back of the trailer. Music out.)*

He's gotta be the biggest boar in the whole world!

ABEL. *(For **MARGY**'s benefit.)* That depends on how ya spell it.

(MELISSA enters in the kitchen with a box, into which she stacks pots and pans.)

Time to hit the road, family. Everybody shake a leg.

MARGY. *(Suddenly enthused, the impending journey now a reality.)* Oh, Harry – we're leaving for the fair! I've gotta finish packing!

(She dashes through the screen door into the kitchen and exits through the archway.)

HARRY. *(Calling after her.)* I'll be waitin' for your answer Saturday night!

(He exits.)

ABEL. Wayne, see if you can hurry your mother along.

(MELISSA crosses resolutely to the cupboard for the brandy.)

WAYNE. *(Entering the kitchen.)* Need a hand with anything, Mom?

MELISSA. *(Slamming the cupboard door shut.)* Well, let me think. You can take that box of pans out for me.

(WAYNE takes the box and crosses out the screen door to the truck.)

[MUSIC NO. 04 "OUR STATE FAIR (REPRISE)"]

(MELISSA takes the brandy from the cupboard and crosses to the crock of mincemeat. She pours in a small amount, then holds the bottle up to see that there are only a few swigs left. With a "now or never" attitude, she empties the remaining brandy into the crock and stirs vigorously.)

ABEL. All aboard that's comin' aboard. Sun's goin' down.

MELISSA. *(Putting the lid on the crock.)* Hurry up, Margy!

> (**MELISSA** *returns the empty bottle to the cupboard, picks up the crock, and crosses out the screen door into the yard.*)

MELISSA. I'll carry this up front.

ABEL. Cover on good and tight?

MELISSA. Certainly it's on tight.

> (*Fearing he might suspect.*)

Why?

ABEL. Wouldn't want any of the flavor to escape, that's all.

> (*Calling into the house.*) Margaret Elizabeth Frake! If I don't get Blue Boy out on the road to cool off...

MARGY. (*Offstage.*) I'm coming!

> (*She sails through the kitchen and onto the porch, singing. Her suitcase has a few sleeves and the hem of a dress hanging out the sides.*)

OUR STATE FAIR IS A GREAT STATE FAIR –
DON'T MISS IT, DON'T EVEN BE LATE.

> (**GUS** *enters, and everyone joins in as they load the last of the provisions onto the truck.*)

ALL.
IT'S DOLLARS TO DOUGHNUTS THAT OUR STATE FAIR
IS THE BEST STATE FAIR IN OUR STATE!

> (*The music continues.*)

ABEL. Hold down the fort, Gus.

GUS. Sure thing, Mr. Frake.

> (**ABEL** *and* **MELISSA** *get into the front seat as* **MARGY** *and* **WAYNE** *jump into the back of the truck.*)

Bring home the bacon!

(A disdainful grunt from Blue Boy in response to this insensitive remark as the truck pulls off upstage. **GUS** *crosses into the kitchen, whistling as he goes. He gleefully takes the brandy bottle from the cupboard, disappointed to find it empty.)*

[MUSIC NO. 05 "DRIVING AT NIGHT / OUR STATE FAIR"]

(The scene shifts to reveal:)

Scene Two
On the Road to Des Moines
Wednesday Morning Before Dawn

(The Frakes' truck appears under a full moon, the music continuing throughout.)

THE FRAKES.
DRIVING AT NIGHT
IN THE COOL OF THE NIGHT,
MOVING EVER FARTHER FROM HOME.
PRETTY SOON WILL BE LIGHT
SHINING EVER SO BRIGHT,
SHINING ON THE CAPITOL DOME,

WHICH MEANS WE'RE
PRACTIC'LLY THERE
AT THE IOWA FAIR.
HAVEN'T HAD THIS FEELING ALL YEAR.
AND NOW IT'S JUST PAST THE BEND,
YES, THE VERY LAST BEND.
KEEP THE OLD JALOPY IN GEAR.

WE'RE HERE! WE'RE HERE!
WE'RE HERE! WE'RE HERE!
WE'RE HERE!

*(As the last note is held, **UNCLE SAM** appears on stilts.)*

UNCLE SAM. Step right up! Welcome to the heart of the Hawkeye State! Welcome to the 1946 Iowa State Fair! Step right up!

(The music continues as the scene shifts to reveal:)

Scene Three
The Midway at the Hoop-La Booth
Later That Morning

(To the cacophony of the **BARKERS'** *overlapping pitches, their booths begin coming into view – the concession stand, the shooting gallery, the Hoop-La booth, and the balloon stand.)*

CONCESSION VENDOR. Step right up! Get your cotton candy, candy apples and salt water taffy! / Step right up! Cotton candy, candy apples and delicious salt water taffy! Sweets for your sweetie right here! Hand-spun cotton candy, hand-dipped candy apples and mouth-watering salt water taffy made fresh all day long! Don't forget to take a box or two home with ya. Sweets for your sweetie right here! Get your cotton candy, candy apples and salt water taffy!

SHOOTING GALLERY BARKER. Step right up, folks, and test your marksmanship. One round of ammo for one thin dime. / Step right up! One round for a dime, three rounds for two bits. Four ducks wins any prize on the shelf. How about you, girlie, if your fella's too shy? Show him how it's done or, better yet, let's have a little shootin' match between the two o' ya. Whaddaya say?

HOOP-LA BARKER. Step right up, ladies and gents! Three rings for a dime – the prize you ring is the prize you get! / Step right up! We're havin' some fun here-ha-ha!

BALLOON VENDOR. Step right up, kids! One balloon for a dime, three for a quarter.

ALL. Step right up!
OUR STATE FAIR IS A GREAT STATE FAIR –
DON'T MISS IT, DON'T EVEN BE LATE!

MEN.
OUR STATE FAIR IS GREAT!

ALL.

> IT'S DOLLARS TO DOUGHNUTS THAT OUR STATE FAIR
> IS THE BEST STATE FAIR IN OUR STATE!

>> (**TWO CLOWNS** – *one dressed as a calf, the other as a piglet – tap dance, delighting the* **CROWD.**)

> OUR STATE FAIR!
> OUR STATE FAIR!
> OUR STATE FAIR!

>> (*Chanting:*)

Our state fair is a great state fair!

Is a great...

Is a great...

Is a great state fair!

Hey!

> OUR STATE FAIR IS A GREAT STATE FAIR –
> DON'T MISS IT, DON'T EVEN BE LATE.
> IT'S DOLLARS TO DOUGHNUTS THAT OUR STATE FAIR
> IS THE BEST STATE FAIR IN OUR STATE!

>> **[MUSIC NO. 06 "MIDWAY CALLIOPE (UNDERSCORE)"]**

>> (*We are on the stretch of midway reserved for the gaming trade. Rides can be seen in the distance, including a Ferris wheel and a death-defying roller coaster. The distinctive voice of the* **FAIR ANNOUNCER** *is heard over the public address system.*)

FAIR ANNOUNCER. (*Offstage.*) Just a reminder, folks – those old gas ration cards are still good for one ride on the Tilt-A-Whirl.

(MARGY and WAYNE enter, MARGY carrying a cone of cotton candy.)

WAYNE. Hey, there's the Hoop-La. C'mon – I feel lucky.

MARGY. We better get over to the roller coaster before the line gets too long.

WAYNE. Roller coaster? Last year you were scared senseless – said you'd never ride it again.

MARGY. Well, that was last year.

WAYNE. I don't wanna go on any stupid rides – kids' stuff.

MARGY. All right, Grampa Moses, you go watch the fertilizer demonstration. I wanna have some fun.

WAYNE. Just be careful. I'm supposed to be keepin' an eye on you.

MARGY. Thank you, big brother. I promise not to have a second cotton candy and run amok.

(She exits. Music out. WAYNE turns his attention to the Hoop-La booth, where the BARKER is giving his pitch to a few prospective CUSTOMERS.)

HOOP-LA BARKER. Step right up, ladies and gents! We're havin' some fun here – ha-ha! Three rings for a dime – the prize you ring is the prize you get! Prizes worth up to fifteen dollars! Ain't nobody got the pioneer spirit? Tell ya what I'll do – I'll put three crisp one-dollar bills down right here...and here...and here.

WAYNE. Is that money real?

HOOP-LA BARKER. If ya don't like 'em, I'll give you a buck apiece for 'em.

(The CROWD chuckles.)

VOICE IN THE CROWD. The hoops don't even fit around those things.

WAYNE. I did it last year. I won a pearl-handled revolver.

HOOP-LA BARKER. Well, now there, ya see? Bring down any grizzly "bars" with that shootin' iron, sonny?

>*(Again the* **CROWD** *chuckles.)*

Now listen here, young Daniel Boone – just to kick things off, I'll give you three rings on the house.

>*(He passes three hoops to* **WAYNE,** *who squares off and takes aim as the* **BARKER** *continues his pitch.)*

I can't win – I can only lose – but I'm only in it for the sport. I love this game!

>*(***WAYNE** *tosses the first hoop and misses.)*

Oops – looks like ya got a little rusty since last year, but then you're just warming up, isn't that right, sonny?

>*(Again the* **CROWD** *chuckles;* **WAYNE**'s *jaw tightens. He pulls himself to his full height and takes aim.)*

Now, who'll be next?

>*(***WAYNE** *tosses the hoop and a bell rings – ding! The surprised* **BARKER** *forces a laugh, handing a dollar bill to* **WAYNE.**)*

Yessiree, Bub, another winner! We're havin' some fun now – ha-ha!

>*(***WAYNE** *tosses the third hoop, and again the bell rings. There's an appreciative murmur from the* **CROWD,** *which is growing larger. The* **BARKER** *begrudgingly hands a second dollar to* **WAYNE.**)*

Ha-ha! I'm down two greenbacks but I'm only in it for the sport of the game! So now that you've all seen how easy it is, who'll be next?

WAYNE. *(Putting his dime on the counter.)* I'll try again.

HOOP-LA BARKER. *(To a* **MAN** *wearing thick glasses.)* How about you, sir? You look like ya got a good eye.

MAN WITH GLASSES. Ya got a customer right there.

A VOICE IN THE CROWD. He's trying to dodge the kid.

ANOTHER VOICE IN THE CROWD. Yeah, he's too good for him.

> *(The* **CROWD** *chuckles.)*

HOOP-LA BARKER. *(Passing three hoops to* **WAYNE**.*)* All right, buddy – here ya go.

(Stepping to the other end of the counter.) Step right up, folks – we're havin' some fun here...!

> *(He's interrupted by the "ding" of the bell.)*

Ha-ha!

(Shoving the third dollar at **WAYNE**.*)* Oh, I love a winner.

(Grabbing **WAYNE***'s arm as he aims.)* Now hold on there, boy – I want you to have a fair shake and that ring looks warped.

> *(He reaches under the counter and brings out another hoop, which he offers to* **WAYNE**.*)*

Here, try this one.

WAYNE. This one's all right.

> *(He takes aim and tosses the hoop; again the bell rings and the* **CROWD** *cheers.)*

HOOP-LA BARKER. *(Handing* **WAYNE** *a vanity case.)* Three bucks and a lovely vanity case but I'm still laughing – ha-ha!

WAYNE. *(Holding up the vanity case to the* **CROWD.***)* Look –
pot metal, molded in one piece. All that stuff's just a lot
o' junk.

HOOP-LA BARKER. Listen, hot shot, I could have you put
in jail for libel – criminal libel! That's right! All I have
to do is call that cop down there.

*(***EMILY ARDEN** *steps out of the* **CROWD.***)*

EMILY. I dare you to call that cop.

*(All heads turn, and an anonymous
wolf-whistle greets this knockout, whose
sophisticated ensemble, picture hat included,
indicates that she's not from around here.)*

(To **WAYNE.***)* He's just trying to bluff you. The law says
he has to sell you all the rings you want. Otherwise, you
can close down his pitch.

HOOP-LA BARKER. Oh, a smart dame, huh? A law student.
Now listen here, arsenic and glamour – I don't know
who you think you are but...

EMILY. I'll tell you who I am. My father is the Chief of
Police and I saw the whole thing.

(Turning to **WAYNE.***)* Say, how'd you get so good?

WAYNE. It's kind of a foolish thing to be good at, isn't it?
But he made me sore last year. I tried for one of those
pearl-handled revolvers. Cost me eight dollars – just
about all I had – and when I finally won, it was just a
toy.

EMILY. Oh, defrauding the public, huh?

(The **CROWD** *murmurs disapprovingly.)*

HOOP-LA BARKER. Now hold on, sister...

WAYNE. I wouldn'ta minded that so much, but he kidded
me in front of the crowd.

EMILY. So you practiced all year to get even.

WAYNE. Figured I'd come back and make as big a fool o' him as he made o' me.

EMILY. Well, it looks like you're doing a pretty fair job.

(The **CROWD** *laughs.)*

(To the **BARKER.***)* Look, if he promises to lay off, will you give him back his eight bucks?

HOOP-LA BARKER. Listen here, Clarence Darrow, I don't care who your father is.

WAYNE. *(Taking aim.)* All right, then...

HOOP-LA BARKER. Okay, okay...

> *(Taking a wad of money from his apron and peeling off some bills.)*

...Here's your lousy eight bucks.

EMILY. *(Snatching the money from the* **BARKER.***)* It's been a pleasure doing business with you. "Ha-ha!"

> *(The* **CROWD** *laughs and begins to disperse as* **EMILY** *hands the money to* **WAYNE.***)*

Don't spend it all in one place.

(She crosses away.)

WAYNE. *(Calling to her.)* Can I buy you a corn dog?

> *(***EMILY** *stops dead in her tracks and turns to him, disbelieving.)*

I mean, it's the least I can do.

EMILY. Maybe next time, Diamond Jim.

WAYNE. The name's Wayne –

(Holding up the money.) – and money's no object. How about a beer instead?

EMILY. Thanks, but it's a little early for cocktails.

WAYNE. *(Feeling stupid.)* Oh...yeah, I guess...

[MUSIC NO. 06A "COOCH DANCE"]

EMILY. Actually, I'm on my way to work. Would you like to walk with me?

WAYNE. Who wouldn't?!

> (**WAYNE** *somewhat self-consciously offers* **EMILY** *his arm, and they exit as the scene shifts to reveal:)*

Scene Four
The Midway at the Temple of Wonder
Immediately Following

(To one side of the stage is the Temple of Wonder, the Test-Your-Strength game to the other side. **FAIRGOERS** *are coming and going as* **THE ASTOUNDING STRALENKO** *gives his pitch on a platform in front of the Temple of Wonder.)*

STRALENKO. Step right up, ladies and gents! Welcome to the Temple of Wonder. Presenting the saucy Siamese twins, Ruth and Esther, and those maidens of Marrakech – Cleopatra's Carnal Cuties!

(He hits a gong; **VIVIAN** *and* **JEANNE,** *two cooch dancers, go into their enticing preview performance.* **PAT GILBERT** *enters, the press pass in his hat indicating that he's a newspaper reporter. He's followed by* **CHARLIE,** *a photographer.)*

PAT. I tell ya, Charlie, I've had some lousy assignments in my day but the old man really stuck me this time.

CHARLIE. He thinks you've gotten too big for your britches so he's taking ya down a peg.

PAT. With what I wrote during the war, for crying-out-loud. I covered Bataan – I covered Midway.

CHARLIE. Yeah, well now you're covering *the* midway. Look, enjoy the sunshine, do your job and shut up about it.

PAT. I got no interest in this human interest junk.

(Music out.)

STRALENKO. And believe me, gentlemen, you'll see a lot *more* of these exotic beauties, but only on the inside. Step right up!

> (**STRALENKO** *exits through a curtain upstage on the platform, followed by* **JEANNE** *and several* **MEN**. **VIVIAN** *calls to* **PAT***:*)

VIVIAN. Hey, Pat! I haven't seen you since V-J Day in Indianapolis! What say we knock back a few after the late show tonight?

PAT. You're on, Valerie.

VIVIAN. It's Vivian.

PAT. Oh, right.

VIVIAN. Same old Pat.

> (*She exits through the curtain.*)

CHARLIE. You must know every dame on the grounds.

PAT. Only the refined typtes.

CHARLIE. I wish I had your knack with women, but I ain't got the gift o' gab. I never know what to say.

PAT. That's easy. Just talk about *them*.

> (**MARGY** *enters.*)

For instance –

> (*He sidles up next to* **MARGY**.)

Say, did you know your hair bounces up and down when you walk?

MARGY. (*Apprehensively.*) Everybody's hair bounces when they walk.

PAT. (*Tipping his hat.*) Mine doesn't.

MARGY. I mean girls.

PAT. On second thought, it's not your hair. It's the way you hold your shoulders.

> (**MARGY** *turns and crosses away;* **PAT** *hurries and steps in front of her.*)

MARGY. *(Nervously.)* Do you always annoy women you don't know?

PAT. Only the beautiful ones, Bobbylocks.

MARGY. Bobbylocks...?

(Getting his reference to her bouncy hair.) I think you have me confused with another type of girl.

PAT. *(Again blocking her path.)* Well now, maybe I do. I had you pegged for the adventurous, sophisticated type, a girl who might be willing to take a chance on a lemonade. You're not afraid of lemonade, are you?

MARGY. No. And I'm not afraid of you either.

PAT. Well that's lucky for you, because you know what they say – "Come the autumn, the robin takes wing. So behold and enjoy the robin in spring."

> (*Flustered,* **MARGY** *looks at him for a long moment.*)

MARGY. Well...thank you for the advice, Mr. Audubon.

PAT. *(Taking her hand and shaking it.)* The name's Pat – Pat Gilbert.

MARGY. It's been nice knowing you, Mr. Gilbert.

> (*She turns to leave, but* **PAT** *doesn't let go of her hand.*)

PAT. And you are...?

MARGY. *(Forcefully pulling her hand from his.)* Leaving.

> (*She exits.*)

CHARLIE. Very smooth, Gilbert.

PAT. Are you kiddin'? She's hooked.

>   *(He exits after* **MARGY.** *A* **GIRL** *crosses, and*
>   **CHARLIE** *calls to her as she exits.)*

CHARLIE. Hey – your hair is really bouncy. Did you know
    that?

>   *(He races off after the* **GIRL** *as* **EMILY** *and*
>   **WAYNE** *enter.)*

WAYNE. But when you're just a little squirt, ya think all
    animals are pets.

>   *(***EMILY** *laughs;* **WAYNE** *pauses.)*

Gosh, I guess I've been talkin' my fool head off.

EMILY. No, I've actually enjoyed it. Thanks for the walk.

>   *(She starts to exit.)*

WAYNE. Listen, can I ask ya something? Back there, at
    the Hoop-La – why'd ya do it? I mean, why would
    somebody like you waste her time on a fella like me
    anyhow?

EMILY. I don't like to see nice guys taken advantage of.
    Besides, what's wrong with you?

WAYNE. There's nothin' wrong with me. Well, maybe there
    is but don't tell me.

EMILY. I better run or I'll be late. See you around.

>   *(She starts to go.)*

WAYNE. When? Where?

EMILY. Oh, I've got a hunch you'll find me.

>   *(She exits, leaving* **WAYNE** *in a state of dazed
>   enchantment, then:)*

WAYNE. Wait – what's your name?

> (*But* **EMILY** *is gone.*)

Wow!

[MUSIC NO. 07 "THAT'S FOR ME"]

RIGHT BETWEEN THE EYES!
QUITE A BELT, THAT BLOW I FELT THIS MORNING!
FATE GAVE ME NO WARNING,
GREAT WAS MY SURPRISE!

I SAW YOU STANDING IN THE SUN,
AND YOU WERE SOMETHING TO SEE!
I KNOW WHAT I LIKE
AND I LIKED WHAT I SAW
AND I SAID TO MYSELF,
"THAT'S FOR ME!"

"A LOVELY MORNING," I REMARKED
AND YOU WERE QUICK TO AGREE,
YOU WANTED TO WALK
AND I NODDED MY HEAD
AS I BREATHLESSLY SAID,
"THAT'S FOR ME!"

YOU LEFT ME STANDING HERE ALONE,
THE DAY'S ADVENTURES ARE THROUGH.
THERE'S NOTHING FOR ME
BUT THE DREAM IN MY HEART,
AND THE DREAM IN MY HEART –
THAT'S FOR YOU!
OH, MY DARLING,
THAT'S FOR YOU!

> (*The music continues as* **WAYNE** *struts over to the Test-Your-Strength game. He tosses the* **BARKER** *a coin, picks up the sledgehammer, lifts it high, brings it crashing down, and rings the bell.*)

WAYNE.
> OH, MY DARLING, THAT'S FOR YOU!

> **[MUSIC NO. 07A "SCENE CHANGE"]**

> *(The* **BARKER** *hands* **WAYNE** *a cigar. He rolls it under his nose, puts it between his teeth, and strolls off confidently as the scene shifts to reveal:)*

Scene Five
The Beer Tent
That Afternoon

FAIR ANNOUNCER. *(Offstage.)* Attention please. Will the parents of little Benny Winkler please claim him at Young McDonald's Farm, and ya better bring a change o' clothes.

> *(ABEL and two fellow farmers – LEM and CLAY – are at a table drinking beer. Each has either a scrapbook or a fistful of snapshots that are being passed around in the spirit of proud parents who only see each other once a year. Music out.)*

ABEL. *(Admiring one of the pictures.)* She's a beauty all right, Lem. How old is she?

LEM. Eighteen months.

ABEL. They grow up so fast, don't they?

HANK. *(Entering.)* Hiya, fellas!

ABEL. Well, if it isn't Hank Munson.

HANK. Well if it isn't, his clothes sure fit me!

> *(He whistles appreciatively at LEM's picture.)*

What a pretty little face.

LEM. She's my pride and joy, Hank – Rosie.

HANK. Well, ya got a fine-lookin' girl there, Lem. Now get a load of my little princess!

> *(He proudly unleashes a long series of photos in a plastic protector that extends the length of the table.)*

LEM. What a snoogams!

CLAY. What a sweetheart!

ABEL. What a sow!

HANK. Isn't she the best-lookin' fat lady you ever saw? That's Esmerelda! We just moved into the pen across from Blue Boy. I tell ya, Abel – he's twice again the boar he was last year.

CLAY. Keep breedin' 'em like that and the bottom's gonna fall out of the pork market.

ABEL. More pig to the pound – that's how they like 'em.

LEM. Ya know one thing I never understood – Virginia ham.

(They all moan knowingly.)

HANK. They don't know how to raise hogs in Virginia!

ABEL. Iowa raises better swine than any state in the Union, and ya know why that is? I'll tell ya why! It's because we know how to treat a pig with the dignity and respect he deserves!

[MUSIC NO. 08 "MORE THAN JUST A FRIEND"]

HANK. Any Iowa farmer worth his salt knows that a hog is more than just livestock.

LEM. Much more. He's a friend.

ABEL.
FRIEND, YOU'RE MORE THAN JUST A FRIEND –
LOYAL, LOVING TO THE END.

ALL. *(In barbershop harmony.)*
SWEET HOG OF MINE,
SWEET HOG OF MINE.

ABEL.
WARM AND SOFT AFFECTION LIES
IN YOUR TEENY-WEENY EYES.

ALL.

    SWEET HOG OF MINE,
    SWEET HOG OF MINE.

ABEL.

    WHEN THE LENGTH'NING SHADOWS FALL
    AND THE DAY IS THROUGH,
    YOU WILL ALWAYS HEAR ME CALL –
    SOO-EY!

HANK.

    SOO-EY!

CLAY.

    SOO-EY!

LEM, CLAY & HANK.

    SA-OO!

ABEL.

    OTHER FRIENDS MAY DRIFT AWAY –
    TELL ME THAT YOU'LL ALWAYS STAY.

ALL.

    SWEET HOG OF MINE,
    SWEET HOG OF MINE.

    SOO-EY!
    SOO-EY!

    WHEN THE LENGTH'NING SHADOWS FALL
    AND THE DAY IS THROUGH,
    YOU WILL ALWAYS HEAR ME CALL –

ABEL.

    SOO-EY!

HANK.

    SOO-EY!

CLAY.

    SOO-EY!

LEM, CLAY & HANK.
SA-OO!
OTHER FRIENDS MAY DRIFT AWAY –
TELL ME THAT YOU'LL ALWAYS STAY.

ABEL.
SWEET HOG OF MINE!

ALL.
SWEET HOG OF MINE!

(A la "Sweet Adeline":)

SWEET HOG OF MINE!

[MUSIC NO. 08A "SCENE CHANGE"]

(The scene shifts to reveal:)

Scene Six
Outside the Dairy Pavilion
Later That Afternoon

(A park bench sits to one side downstage of the entrance to the Dairy Pavilion. **FAIRGOERS** *are coming and going, including an eager* **COUPLE** *headed toward the Dairy Pavilion; they stop to listen to the announcement.)*

FAIR ANNOUNCER. *(Offstage.)* Attention please. Due to a refrigeration breakdown, there will be no butter sculpture of "The Last Supper."

(The disappointed **COUPLE** *exits as* **PAT** *and* **MARGY** *enter. Music out.)*

PAT. So where to now, Bobbylocks? And please – anything but the roller coaster again.

MARGY. I could ride all day, given half a chance.

(They sit on the bench.)

PAT. The one in Chicago – now that's a roller coaster. The one at Coney Island's pretty good, and there's one on the beach near LA that's not bad, but the one in Chicago – that's the one! Got a dip of two hundred feet.

MARGY. You've been everywhere, haven't you?

PAT. Seen it all, done it all.

(He chuckles.)

No, I haven't. When I first started out in this racket I worked on different papers all over the country. Got a couple lucky breaks as a war correspondent – wrote some good stuff, got some attention. Not that it ever led to anything much, the way I thought it would. Now I'm stuck at United Press. I used to think that someday I'd land a real job on a real paper.

MARGY. Have you tried?

PAT. I put out a few feelers – sent some letters.

MARGY. I don't mean writing letters. I mean writing more good stories that get more attention.

PAT. My boss hasn't exactly been handing me the plumb assignments lately.

MARGY. You're covering the fair, aren't you?

PAT. Like I said.

MARGY. Are you kidding? This is the biggest story in the world! Well, my world anyway. The fair is all about the land and nature – it's about people taking pride in what we do with our lives. Well, what could be more interesting to write about than that?

[MUSIC NO. 09 "ISN'T IT KINDA FUN?"]

PAT. I like you, Margy Frake.

MARGY. Well...I like you too, but we hardly know each other.

PAT. Maybe hardly knowing each other isn't so bad.

MAYBE YOU'LL NEVER BE THE LOVE OF MY LIFE,
MAYBE I'M NOT THE BOY OF YOUR DREAMS,
BUT ISN'T IT KINDA FUN TO LOOK IN EACH OTHER'S EYES,
SWAPPING ROMANTIC GLEAMS?

MAYBE YOU'RE NOT A GIRL TO HAVE AND TO HOLD,
MAYBE I'M NOT A BOY WHO WOULD STAY,
BUT ISN'T IT KINDA FUN CAROUSING AROUND THE TOWN,
DANCING THE NIGHT AWAY?

ISN'T IT KINDA FUN HOLDING HANDS,
ACCORDING TO A SWEET AND CORNY CUSTOM?
ISN'T IT KINDA FUN MAKING VOWS,
ADMITTING THAT WE BOTH INTEND TO BUST 'EM!

MAYBE WE'RE OUT FOR LAUGHS, A GIRL AND A BOY,
KIDDING ACROSS A TABLE FOR TWO,

BUT HAVEN'T YOU GOT A HUNCH THAT THIS IS THE REAL
    MCCOY
AND ALL THE THINGS WE TELL EACH OTHER ARE TRUE?

MARGY.

I'M NOT A GIRL FOR SENTIMENTAL TRIPE,
I NEVER GO FOR THE ROMEO TYPE.

PAT.

OVER A DEWY-EYED JULIET
NO ONE HAS SEEN ME DROOL YET.

MARGY.

I DON'T SAY OUR HEARTS ARE TIED BY
LOVE'S ETERNAL TETHER.

PAT.

BUT USING WORDS LESS DIGNIFIED,
ISN'T IT KINDA FUN TO BE TOGETHER?
MAYBE WE'RE OUT FOR LAUGHS, A GIRL AND A BOY,
KIDDING ACROSS A TABLE FOR TWO.

PAT & MARGY.

BUT HAVEN'T YOU GOT A HUNCH THAT THIS IS THE REAL
    MCCOY
AND ALL THE THINGS WE TELL EACH OTHER ARE TRUE?[*]

*(They dance a flirtatious game of cat and
mouse, and end with a handshake.)*

PAT. Say, can I see ya tomorrow?

MARGY. Well, I...

PAT. Or do you wanna call it quits?

---

[*]Alternate ending:
PAT.
BUT HAVEN'T YOU GOT A HUNCH THAT THIS IS THE REAL MCCOY,
AND THAT THE THINGS WE TELL EACH OTHER
PAT & MARGY.
ARE TRUE.

MARGY. No! I mean...well, do you?

PAT. Look, Bobbylocks, any time I wanna call it quits, you won't have to ask – I just won't be around. So do we have a date?

MARGY. Well, tomorrow afternoon my mother's pickles and mincemeat are being judged.

PAT. They can't give 'em more than thirty days unless they're guilty of a felony. So what time do they sentence those condiments?

MARGY. Three o'clock,

PAT. Three o'clock it is.

> *(He moves toward her.)*

MARGY. I should be getting back.

PAT. Can I walk ya home?

MARGY. Well...I'm afraid I'd have a hard time explaining you to my parents.

PAT. Everybody has a hard time explaining me. Then I'll just say so long for now.

> *(He extends his hand, and* **MARGY** *shakes it.)*

MARGY. So long, Pat – and thanks.

[MUSIC NO. 10 "END OF SCENE SIX"]

> *(***PAT*** *exits, and* **MARGY** *stands silent for a moment, absolutely charmed.)*

MAYBE WE'RE OUT FOR LAUGHS, A GIRL AND A BOY,
KIDDING ACROSS A TABLE FOR TWO,
BUT HAVEN'T YOU GOT A HUNCH THAT THIS IS THE REAL MCCOY
AND ALL THE THINGS WE TELL EACH OTHER...

(She stops herself, feeling silly for getting carried away.)

Oh, Margy...

(She exits as the scene shifts to reveal:)

Scene Seven
The Starlight Dance Meadow
That Night

(This romantic, open-air dance pavilion has café tables and chairs bordering the dance floor, a "stage" for the entertainment, and a bar upstage. **COUPLES** *are dancing and spirits are high as* **WAYNE** *enters downstage. He sees the* **CHIEF OF POLICE** *and crosses to him.)*

WAYNE. Excuse me, sir – are you the Chief of Police?

CHIEF. That's right, son. What can I do for ya?

WAYNE. Well, I was wondering if...that is, could you tell me where your daughter is?

CHIEF. My daughter?

WAYNE. Yeah, we sort of had a date to...

CHIEF. A what?

WAYNE. Well, it wasn't exactly a date, sir, but she said... I mean, we sort of arranged...

CHIEF. Well, if you say so.

(Looking off and calling.) Violet? She's around here someplace. Violet?

*(**WAYNE** straightens himself expectantly; his face goes blank as **VIOLET** enters. She is only about eleven years old, all pigtails and freckles.)*

VIOLET. Yes, Daddy?

CHIEF. This young man tells me you two have plans to step out tonight.

VIOLET. *(Love at first sight!)* Really? Hot dog!

WAYNE. *(Clearly embarrassed.)* I think I mean your older daughter.

VIOLET. Haven't got a sister, good-lookin'. You mean me!

CHIEF. Looks like somebody's been pullin' your leg, son.

WAYNE. *(Laughing half-heartedly.)* Yeah, I guess that's a hot one on me. Well...I...er...

(Shaking **VIOLET***'s hand.)* Nice meeting you.

(To the **CHIEF.***)* Thanks.

> *(He crosses away,* **VIOLET** *dogging him step for step. He stops and turns to her.)*

Look, little girl, we don't really have a date. It was a joke.

VIOLET. Do you see me laughing?

> *(The music ends and the* **CROWD** *applauds as* **WAYNE** *crosses and sits at a table downstage, followed by* **VIOLET***, who takes the seat across from him.)*

EMCEE. *(Offstage.)* Ladies and gentlemen, the Starlight Dance Meadow is proud to present Emily Arden and The Fairtones.

> **[MUSIC NO. 11 "YOU NEVER HAD IT SO GOOD"]**

> *(***EMILY** *enters onto the "stage.")*

EMILY.
YOU NEVER HAD IT SO GOOD –
FOR ONCE IN YOUR LIFE, YOU'RE LIVING.
SHOW YOUR BABY YOU'RE GRATEFUL
FOR ALL YOUR BABY IS GIVING.

> *(The* **CHIEF** *signals* **VIOLET** *away from the table, and they exit.* **WAYNE** *turns and sees*

> **EMILY** *for the first time; he jumps to his feet, grinning ear to ear as if to say, "I know that girl!")*

EMILY.
YOU NEVER HAD IT SO GOOD –
YOU CRAZY, ATTRACTIVE MUG, YOU.
SHOW YOUR BABY YOU'RE GRATEFUL
OR BABY IS GOING TO SLUG YOU!

> **(THE FAIRTONES** *enter, four boys who back her up.)*

EMILY.	**THE FAIRTONES.**
I'LL SEW, I'LL BAKE, I'LL TRY TO MAKE	OO
YOUR EVENINGS ALL ENCHANTED.	
MY HONEY CAKE, I'M YOURS TO TAKE	
BUT DON'T TAKE ME FOR GRANTED.	
JUST DO WHAT ANYONE WOULD –	
CONFESS YOU'RE A LUCKY FELLER,	LUCKY
COME TO BABY AND TELL HER	GUY!
	YOU TELL HER!
YOU'VE BEEN MISUNDERSTOOD.	
KISS YOUR BABY AND TELL HER	
	TELL HER!
YOU NEVER HAD IT SO GOOD,	
SO GOOD!	SO GOOD!

I'LL SEW, I'LL BAKE, I'LL
    TRY TO MAKE   OO
YOUR EVENINGS ALL
    ENCHANTED.

EMILY & THE FAIRTONES.
MY HONEY CAKE, I'M YOURS TO TAKE
BUT DON'T TAKE ME FOR GRANTED.

EMILY.
JUST DO WHAT ANYONE
    WOULD   **THE FAIRTONES.**
CONFESS YOU'RE A LUCKY   FELLER,
    FELLER,
COME TO BABY AND TELL
    HER   YOU
                       TELL HER!
YOU'VE BEEN   YOU'VE BEEN
    MISUNDERSTOOD.   MISUNDERSTOOD
KISS YOUR BABY AND TELL   KISS AND TELL HER IT'S
    HER
YOU NEVER HAD IT SO   SO GOOD, SO GOOD.
    GOOD,
SO GOOD!   SO GOOD!

EMILY. *(In tempo.)* Hello, boys.

THE FAIRTONES. Hey, Miss Arden.

> (**EMILY** *and* **THE FAIRTONES** *go into a rousing dance routine. At the conclusion of the number, the* **CROWD** *applauds as* **EMILY** *and* **THE FAIRTONES** *take their bows.* **THE FAIRTONES** *exit.)*

> **[MUSIC NO. 11A "THAT'S FOR DANCING"]**

> (*A few* **COUPLES** *get up to dance as* **EMILY** *crosses to* **WAYNE**, *who rises to greet her.)*

EMILY. I told you you'd find me.

WAYNE. I didn't know you were a celebrity.

EMILY. Few people do.

>   *(Pause.)*

Can I sit down?

WAYNE. Oh, yeah...sorry.

>   *(He pulls the chair out for* **EMILY,** *then sits across from her.)*

I had a nice talk with your father on my way in.

EMILY. My father?

WAYNE. You know – the Chief of Police?

EMILY. Oh, that gag's so old it's got whiskers. You didn't actually fall for it, did you?

WAYNE. Yeah, I guess so. But I did get to meet the chief's daughter. Interesting girl – pretty. In fact, I think she kinda went for me.

EMILY. I'm sure she did.

WAYNE. There's only one catch.

EMILY. What's that?

WAYNE. She's eleven.

EMILY. *(Laughing.)* Oh, no! I'm really sorry. Listen, you're such a good sport – can I buy you a beer?

WAYNE. You bet.

EMILY. *(To the* **BARTENDER.***)* A couple of drafts, Eddie.

BARTENDER. Comin' up.

EMILY. So, tell me more about the farm.

WAYNE. Oh, you're not interested in all that. It's just a farm.

EMILY. The closest I ever got to a farm was our fifth-floor walk-up in Detroit. We had a window box of geraniums.

WAYNE. When did you move to Des Moines?

EMILY. I'm just here working. Last week Grand Rapids, next week Milwaukee.

WAYNE. Don't ya get lonely, being away from your family so much?

EMILY. Family? Well, there are a few people back in Detroit, but they don't really know me anymore. I never look back, only forward. Actually, I'm headed for New York.

WAYNE. New York *City*? Why?

EMILY. Well, in all modesty, I'm going to be a star. You know – on Broadway.

WAYNE. Really? Say, what's your name anyhow?

EMILY. Emily. Emily Arden.

WAYNE. *(Holding his hands up as if framing a marquee.)* "Emily Arden." I can just see it in lights.

EMILY. So can I. What I couldn't see in lights was Emma Kozlowski. So, how long are you here for?

WAYNE. We head back to Brunswick Saturday morning.

    (Music out.)

Maybe we could get together again – sometime when you're not working?

EMILY. I'd like that, Wayne, but let's make sure we understand each other first.

WAYNE. Whaddaya mean?

EMILY. First rule of show business – always leave 'em laughing. Nothing complicated, okay?

WAYNE. Oh sure, of course – nothing complicated.

    (They lift their mugs in a toast as the band strikes up another tune.)

[MUSIC NO. 11B "SCENE CHANGE"]

EMILY. Do you like to dance?

WAYNE. You bet. Do you?

EMILY. *(Referring to the knock-down, drag-out dance routine she just did.)* Couldn't you tell?

> *(She leads* **WAYNE** *onto the floor and they disappear among the* **DANCING COUPLES** *as the scene shifts to reveal:)*

Scene Eight
Camper's Hill
Thursday Morning

(The Frakes' campsite is on a hilltop overlooking the fairgrounds. Two tents are pitched upstage – one for Wayne and Abel, the other for Margy and Melissa. Downstage is a picnic table, a water spigot, and a grill. The back end of the truck juts onstage to one side, in which MELISSA *has arranged her pots and pans, dishes, and other supplies.* MELISSA *is at the table washing the last of the breakfast dishes in a wash basin while* MARGY *dries and stacks them. Music out.)*

MELISSA. I wish your father would get back here. My world does not revolve around Blue Boy. I've got my whole day planned out.

MARGY. You can't plan out a whole day.

MELISSA. I do it all the time.

MARGY. You sound like Harry. He thinks you can plan out your whole life.

MELISSA. So you can.

(Casually.) Is that what you two were talking about the other day?

MARGY. Yep.

MELISSA. Did you come to anything definite?

MARGY. Nope.

MELISSA. *(Exasperated.)* I'm sure I don't know what you're waiting for. I mean, what's wrong with Harry?

MARGY. There's nothing wrong with him. I'm just not sure I want the kind of life Harry has all planned out for us.

[MUSIC NO. 12 "IT MIGHT AS WELL BE SPRING (REPRISE)"]

MARGY.

> IN OUR AIR-CONDITIONED, PATENT LEATHER FARMHOUSE
> ON OUR ULTRA-MODERN, SCIENTIFIC FARM,
> WE'LL LIVE IN A STREAMLINED HEAVEN
>
> AND WE'LL WASTE NO TIME ON CHARM.
> NO GERANIUMS TO CLUTTER OUR VERANDA,
> NOR A SINGLE LITTLE SENTIMENTAL THING.
> NO VIRGINIA CREEPERS – NOTHING USELESS...

> *(The music continues.)*

MELISSA. Harry would make a perfectly respectable husband. Lord knows, he's been patient with you. It'd serve you right if he up and married that McCaskey girl instead of you – and I almost hope he does.

MARGY. Me too.

MELISSA. Oh, Margy... Ya know, Harry's not gonna wait around forever.

MARGY. I promised Harry an answer after the fair.

MELISSA. Oh?

MARGY. Three days. How am I supposed to decide the rest of my life in three days? There's so much I haven't done yet, so much I haven't seen.

> I KEEP WISHING I WERE SOMEWHERE ELSE,
> WALKING DOWN A STRANGE NEW STREET,
> HEARING WORDS THAT I HAVE NEVER HEARD
> FROM A MAN I'VE YET TO MEET.

> *(**WAYNE** enters cheerfully, unseen by **MARGY**. He's wearing his undershirt and has a towel around his neck.)*

HE WOULD BE A KIND OF HANDSOME COMBINATION
OF RONALD COLMAN, CHARLES BOYER AND BING...

*(WAYNE tosses the towel over MARGY's head.
Music out.)*

WAYNE. Good morning, beautiful sister.

MARGY. *(Throwing the towel at him.)* Honestly, Wayne...

WAYNE. Good morning, beautiful mother.

(He gives MELISSA a kiss on the cheek.)

MELISSA. Well, you certainly must've had a good time last
night.

WAYNE. Oh, we had a swell time.

(With a look to MARGY.) Didn't *we*, Margy.

MARGY. Oh...yeah! The two of us, together – terrific time.

*(WAYNE exits into the tent as MARGY and
MELISSA fold the tablecloth.)*

MELISSA. You certainly are gussied up just to walk the
midway.

MARGY. Well...the midway's very dressy this year.

(ABEL enters.)

ABEL. I am here to tell ya, Blue Boy's the best-lookin' piece
o' hog flesh in the Hawkeye State!

MELISSA. Did you drop off my pickles and mincemeat?

ABEL. All signed in and delivered.

*(WAYNE emerges from the tent, now wearing
a shirt.)*

Now, seeing as how this is Mother's big day, I'm gonna
take the family out tonight.

[MUSIC NO. 13 "WHEN I GO OUT WALKING WITH MY BABY"]

ABEL. Dinner, dancing, the whole nine yards!

MELISSA. *(Extremely pleased.)* Oh, Abel – dancing?

ABEL. *(Crossing to her and putting his arm around her waist.)* You heard me.

WHEN I GO OUT WALKING WITH MY BABY,
STARS ARE DANCIN' IN MY BABY'S EYES!

MELISSA.

WHEN I DO THE CAKEWALK WITH MY BABY,
ME AND MY BABY ALWAYS WIN THE PRIZE!

ABEL.

WHEN I TAKE HER HOME WE START IN SPOONIN',

MELISSA.

SPOONIN' SUITS MY BABY TO A "T."

ABEL & MELISSA.

PRETTY SOON YOU'RE GOING TO SEE SOME
    HONEYMOONIN',
'CAUSE IF I DON'T MARRY HER (HIM), SHE'LL (HE'LL)
    MARRY ME!

ABEL. *(To **MARGY** and **WAYNE**.)* Watch and learn.

> *(**ABEL** leads **MELISSA** in a genteel dance to the ragtime rhythm. The following lines are spoken during their dance.)*

Easy, Mother – don't give it all away.

> *(The dance continues.)*

Hold on tight.

MELISSA. Every chance I get.

> *(The dance continues, becoming more exuberant.)*

ABEL. We may not strut it out often, but we still got it!

> (**MELISSA** *does the shimmy.*)

Don't taunt me, woman!

> (*The dance continues.*)

Let's bring it home, Mother!

> (*They pull out all the stops as the number concludes.*)

[MUSIC NO. 13A "PLAYOFF INTO PICKLES"]

C'mon, kids – let's see if ya can keep up.

> (*The* **FRAKES** *exit doing the cakewalk as the scene shifts to reveal:*)

Scene Nine
Exhibition Hall
That Afternoon

FAIR ANNOUNCER. *(Offstage.)* Just a reminder, folks – following the pickles and mincemeats, they'll be judgin' piccalilli, chutney and chow-chow.

> *(The music continues. Downstage is a platform with a few steps leading up to it from either side. The back of the platform is lined with shelves containing various food items in mason jars and crocks. Three* **JUDGES** – **MR. HEPPENSTAHL**, *who is the head judge, one* **LADY**, *and another* **GENTLEMAN** – *stand behind a counter which displays several jars of pickles; each* **JUDGE** *holds a pickle on a fork.* **TWO ASSISTANTS** *stand to one side, one holding an atomizer, the other a small tin pail. Each* **JUDGE** *takes a bite of his/her respective pickle, savoring, none too subtly, the many nuances of its flavor. The* **ASSISTANT** *with the pail crosses past the* **JUDGES** *as they consecutively spit the chewed pickle into the pail. [The* **ASSISTANT** *"plunks" the bottom of the pail as each* **JUDGE** *spits, effecting the sound of the chewed pickle landing in the pail. See "spit" cues in score.] The* **ASSISTANT** *with the atomizer follows, spraying into the open mouth of each* **JUDGE**, *who then takes a napkin from the table to dab his/her mouth. Among the* **SPECTATORS** *are the* **FRAKES** *on one side of the stage and* **MRS. METCALF**, *a snooty matron, and her* **FRIENDS** *on the other.* **CHARLIE** *is also present to one side;* **PAT** *enters to him.)*

PAT. Hiya, shutterbug. Sorry I'm late.

CHARLIE. So tell me, which dainty homemaker is the cause of our presence here?

PAT. Have you ever known me to go for the type that cooks?

CHARLIE. You've gone for every other type – it was only a matter of time. Say, before I forget –

(Taking a Western Union envelope from his pocket.) This wire came for you.

PAT. Uh-oh, who died?

(He opens it and reads. Music out.)

HEPPENSTAHL. Ladies and gentlemen, we have completed the pickles and will now move on to the mincemeats, after which time the winners in both categories will be announced.

(The ASSISTANTS clear the pickle jars from the table to the shelves and replace them with crocks as the JUDGES turn upstage to confer.)

PAT. Eureka! There's an opening on the Chicago Tribune – the managing editor wants to see me Monday for an interview!

CHARLIE. *(Slapping PAT on the back.)* There ya go! Looks like this could be your ticket out.

PAT. Charlie, if I was to dream up something I wanted, I couldn't do better than this.

(The JUDGES begin tasting the mincemeats.)

MRS. METCALF'S FRIEND. So, Mrs. Metcalf, going to win all the prizes again this year?

MRS. METCALF. *(Grandly.)* Well, I *have* been winning both pickles and mincemeat for so many years now that I'm almost embarrassed.

(She and her FRIENDS laugh giddily.)

MARGY. *(Clutching her mother's arm.)* Don't pay any attention to that pompous old biddy!

ABEL. She thinks she's the only one who knows her way around a cucumber.

MELISSA. *(Rigid with suspense and worry, fanning herself with the fair schedule.)* This is the last year I enter anything and I mean it.

MARGY. Oh, you say that every year.

ABEL. Now hold tight, Mother. They're comin' up to yours and I got a hunch it's gonna send 'em to the promised land!

> *(The* **JUDGES** *each dip into* **MELISSA**'*s crock with a small spoon and take a taste, their eyes widening with delight. They share a look and immediately dig in for another spoonful; they smack their lips in unison. The* **LADY** *and* **GENTLEMAN JUDGE** *turn upstage to confer while* **HEPPENSTAHL** *hangs over the crock, shoveling in spoonful after spoonful.)*

WAYNE. They must like it – they sure are wolfin' it down.

> *(The* **ASSISTANT** *offers* **HEPPENSTAHL** *the pail, which he pushes away, continuing to eat the mincemeat. He lets escape an involuntary belch, much to the disdain of the* **LADY JUDGE**, *who indicates that he join them in deliberating. The* **JUDGES** *confer.* **HEPPENSTAHL** *turns to the noisy* **CROWD** *and loudly clears his throat for their attention.)*

HEPPENSTAHL. Ah-hum –

> *(An instant hush falls over the* **CROWD** *as they turn to him in rapt attention.)*

We are now ready to announce the winners. Sweet pickles. Second place to...Mrs. Dorothy Saxhorn of Osceola.

> *(Applause from the* **CROWD** *as she receives her red ribbon.)*

And first place to...Mrs. Edwin Metcalf of Pottsville.

> *(Applause, especially animated from* **MRS. METCALF'S FRIENDS,** *as she receives her blue ribbon with a haughty wave of her hand to the* **CROWD. HEPPENSTAHL** *is by now in fine fettle, the effects of the brandy becoming apparent.)*

And moving right along to sour pickles! Second place to...Mrs. Melissa Frake of Brunswick.

> *(Applause from the* **CROWD** *as* **MELISSA** *receives her red ribbon.)*

And first place to...Mrs. Edwin Metcalf!

> *(Applause as she receives her second blue ribbon.* **HEPPENSTAHL** *is becoming somewhat boisterous.)*

I'm beginning to sound like a broken record, aren't I, Mrs. Metcalf?

> *(He laughs uproariously, but the* **LADY JUDGE** *throws him a dirty look and he shapes up.)*

Oh, yes, now where were we? Oh yes, the mincemeats!

MELISSA. *(Fanning herself wildly and squeezing* **MARGY**'s *hand.)* Oh, goodness, I don't think I can take it.

HEPPENSTAHL. Second place to...Mrs. Robert Mosely of Cedar Bluff!

> *(Applause as she receives her red ribbon.)*

MELISSA. Well, it looks like a clean sweep for the Metcalf woman again.

ABEL. Now hold your horses, Mother. It ain't over yet.

*(Having quickly scarfed down one more spoonful of mincemeat, **HEPPENSTAHL** returns to the microphone, now clearly tipsy.)*

HEPPENSTAHL. And first place goes to...

(He pauses importantly.)

Ladies and gentlemen, as you know, we occasionally give a plaque for distinguished achievement in the culinary arts.

(A murmur of excitement runs through the **CROWD.***)*

As you are undoubtlessly aware, this plaque is only given in the rarest of shircum...circue...we don't give it out much. On this occasion, my colleagues and I have voted *umaminously* that it be given to a lady who has concocted the most delicious, the most succulent mincemeat ever to grace our State Fair! The lady who wins this Plaque of Distinction is none other than... Mrs. Melissa Brake of Frunswick!

(The **CROWD** *applauds as* **MELISSA** *steps forward, and the* **ASSISTANT** *hands her the plaque and a blue ribbon.)*

Congratulations, Mrs. France. And congratulations to all of our winners.

ABEL. What'd I tell you!

MELISSA. It's unbelievable! If I think anymore about it, I'll just cry.

(The **CROWD** *is dispersing;* **MRS. METCALF** *addresses* **MELISSA** *on her way out.)*

MRS. METCALF. Congratulations, Mrs. Frake. After trying and failing over and over again, year after year... Well, it just does my heart good to see you finally achieve some small token of recognition.

MELISSA. *(Genuinely honored.)* Why, thank you, Mrs. Metcalf.

ABEL. And congratulations to you. You certainly know your sour pickles.

>   (**MRS. METCALF** *exits as* **PAT** *and* **CHARLIE** *approach.)*

PAT. Congratulations, Mrs. Frake. We're with United Press. Can we get a shot?

MELISSA. Well...I...er...

ABEL. You're a celebrity now, Mother. Don't hide your light under a basket.

PAT. *(To* **CHARLIE.***)* How about a shot of the whole family, Charlie?

CHARLIE. Why not? Now, Mrs. Frake...

(Leading her into position.) Let's have you right here in front. And Mr. Frake, you get in here next to the champ.

PAT. *(Gingerly guiding* **MARGY** *into position.)* Miss Frake, let's get you in here on the other side of your mother...

(Indicating **WAYNE** *without taking his eyes off* **MARGY.***)* And your brother there in the back somewhere. Charlie, can we get the Crock of Distinction in here?

CHARLIE. Why not?

>   (**CHARLIE** *reaches for the crock, but* **HEPPENSTAHL** *holds on tight, threatening him with his raised spoon.)*

Look, pal, I'm not taking it across the border – it's just a picture.

(**HEPPENSTAHL** *looks to* **MELISSA** *and melts, overcome in the presence of this domestic goddess. He releases the crock with a little wave of his fingers to* **MELISSA**, *who returns the gesture uncertainly.* **CHARLIE** *hands the crock to* **MELISSA**.)

CHARLIE. Here ya go.

(**CHARLIE** *backs up and aims his camera.*)

Now, let's have a big smile – everybody say "cheese."

(*Everyone says "cheese,"* **HEPPENSTAHL** *included, and* **CHARLIE** *takes the picture.*)

PAT. That's just fine, folks. Thanks a lot.

(**HEPPENSTAHL** *snatches the crock from* **MELISSA** *and exits upstage behind the judges' platform.*)

MELISSA. Thank you, Mr...

(**PAT** *and* **MARGY** *answer simultaneously.*)

PAT & MARGY. Gilbert.

(**MARGY**'s *afraid she's let the cat out of the bag, but* **PAT** *jumps right in.*)

PAT. That's right, Pat Gilbert.

(*He shakes* **MELISSA**'s *hand with a smile to* **MARGY**.)

Congratulations again. C'mon, Charlie – we'd better get over to the Dairy Pavilion.

CHARLIE. (*With a knowing look to* **MARGY**.) Why not?

(**PAT** *and* **CHARLIE** *exit.*)

MELISSA. What a nice fella, and handsome, too. Don't you think, Margy?

MARGY. *(Too ingenuous.)* Is he? I guess I didn't notice.

MELISSA. Really? I did.

>*(Meaning that she noticed exactly how* **MARGY** *didn't notice.)*

ABEL. Well, c'mon now – we better check in on Blue Boy. Ya know how surly he gets if he thinks somebody else is gettin' all the attention. Ya comin', Wayne?

WAYNE. I...er... Jeez, I signed up for the tractor pull. I better get goin' or I'll be late.

>*(***WAYNE*** *hurries off.)*

ABEL. Margy?

MARGY. Um... I'm gonna run over to the Dairy Pavilion. I promised Betty Bugowski I'd cheer her on in the Ice Cream Crank-off.

>*(She hurries off in the same direction* **PAT** *went.)*

MELISSA. Well, I am absolutely done in. It's funny – I never realized what a strain it is to actually get something you've only dreamed of.

ABEL. Now when Blue Boy holds up his end of the bargain tomorrow, it'll be a clean sweep for the Frakes of Brunswick – and Dave Miller's gonna owe me five bucks!

[MUSIC NO. 13B "SCENE CHANGE"]

>*(***MELISSA*** *and* **ABEL** *exit as the platform moves off, revealing* **HEPPENSTAHL**, *still eating out of the crock. He staggers off as the scene shifts to reveal:)*

Scene Ten
A Nearby Hillside
Early That Night

(To one side is a large, raised clearing.
WAYNE *and* **EMILY** *stroll on. Music out.*
There's a moment of nervous silence with
only the sound of crickets chirping in the
background.)

WAYNE. Ever heard of cow tipping?

EMILY. Okay, I'll bite. What does a cow do to earn a tip?

WAYNE. No, it's not that, it's… Cows sleep standing up
sometimes – when they're grazing – and if ya sneak up
on 'em, ya can push 'em over.

EMILY. *(Getting it.)* Cow tipping!

WAYNE. Cow tipping.

(Another awkward silence.)

Gee, it's beautiful up here. Nice to get away from the
folks for a while.

EMILY. Sounds like a nice family. You're lucky.

WAYNE. Yeah, they're okay, if ya like family. They do
tend to get in the way sometimes, though. I told 'em I
entered the tractor pull and now I'll have to come up
with some cock and bull story about why I didn't win.

EMILY. Just tell 'em the tractor pulled harder.

*(**WAYNE** restrains himself from correcting her*
impression of what a tractor pull really is.)

WAYNE. Ya know, tomorrow's the last day of the fair and
this is the first time we've had two minutes alone
together.

EMILY. Look, Wayne, you've got this sweet little family and I've got a bus ticket to Milwaukee. You're headed back to the farm and I'm headed for the Big Apple. You're just a little bit over twenty-one and I'm just a little bit... more over twenty-one.

WAYNE. Why should that matter?

EMILY. Maybe I've had too much experience beginning things I couldn't finish.

WAYNE. Who cares about the past? I thought you said you never looked back – only forward.

[MUSIC NO. 14 "SO FAR"]

NO KEEPSAKES HAVE WE
FOR DAYS THAT ARE GONE,
NO FOND RECOLLECTIONS
TO LOOK BACK UPON,
NO SONGS THAT WE LOVE,
NO SCENE TO RECALL –
WE HAVE NO TRADITIONS AT ALL.

WE HAVE NOTHING TO REMEMBER SO FAR, SO FAR –
SO FAR WE HAVEN'T WALKED BY NIGHT
AND SHARED THE LIGHT OF A STAR.
SO FAR YOUR HEART HAS NEVER FLUTTERED SO NEAR –
    SO NEAR
THAT MY OWN HEART ALONE COULD HEAR IT.

WE HAVEN'T GONE BEYOND THE VERY BEGINNING.
WE'VE JUST BEGUN TO KNOW HOW LUCKY WE ARE.
SO WE HAVE NOTHING TO REMEMBER SO FAR, SO FAR –
BUT NOW I'M FACE TO FACE WITH YOU
AND NOW AT LAST WE'VE MET,
AND NOW WE CAN LOOK FORWARD TO
THE THINGS WE'LL NEVER FORGET.

> *(The music continues as they tentatively kiss.*
> **EMILY** *pulls from him and crosses away.)*

WAYNE. What's wrong?

EMILY. First rule of show business, remember? We made a
    deal to play this strictly for laughs – nothing complicated.
    I don't want to drag you in over your head, Wayne.

WAYNE. It's too late for that. I'm already in, head over
    heels.

EMILY.

WE HAVEN'T GONE BEYOND THE VERY BEGINNING,
WE'VE JUST BEGUN TO KNOW HOW LUCKY WE ARE.

EMILY & WAYNE.

SO WE HAVE NOTHING TO REMEMBER SO FAR, SO FAR –
BUT NOW I'M FACE TO FACE WITH YOU
AND NOW AT LAST WE'VE MET,
AND NOW WE CAN LOOK FORWARD TO
THE THINGS WE'LL NEVER FORGET.

>   (**EMILY** *leads* **WAYNE** *to the clearing as the
>   music segues directly into:*)

>   **[MUSIC NO. 15 "IT'S A GRAND NIGHT FOR
>   SINGING (FINALE ACT I)"]**

>   (**EMILY** *pulls* **WAYNE** *down into her embrace
>   and they kiss passionately. A* **COUPLE** *dances
>   across upstage;* **ANOTHER COUPLE** *dances on,
>   then* **ANOTHER COUPLE** *as the scene shifts to
>   reveal:*)

>   (**COUPLES** *are dancing and romance is in the
>   air.* **PAT** *is at the bar upstage.*)

ALL.

IT'S A GRAND NIGHT FOR SINGING!
THE MOON IS FLYING HIGH,
AND SOMEWHERE A BIRD
WHO IS BOUND HE'LL BE HEARD
IS THROWING HIS HEART AT THE SKY.

IT'S A GRAND NIGHT FOR SINGING!
THE STARS ARE BRIGHT ABOVE,
THE EARTH IS AGLOW
AND TO ADD TO THE SHOW,
I THINK I AM FALLING IN LOVE –
FALLING, FALLING IN LOVE!

> *(The music continues as* **ABEL**, **MELISSA**, *and* **MARGY** *enter.)*

MELISSA. Oh, Abel, isn't it lovely?

ABEL. Pretty as a picture.

> *(***PAT*** crosses down to the* **FRAKES**.*)*

PAT. Good evening, folks. Enjoying the music?

MELISSA. Good evening, Mr. Gilbert.

ABEL. Yes, fine band.

PAT. Would you like to dance, Miss Frake?

MARGY. *(A bit flustered.)* Well...um...

ABEL. Go on, honey – live it up a little.

MARGY. Why, thank you, Mr. Gilbert.

> *(***PAT*** leads her onto the floor.)*

How did you know I'd be here?

PAT. I'm a reporter. It's my job to find people.

> *(They join in the dance as* **HEPPENSTAHL** *enters, still tipsy. He spots* **MELISSA** *and waves to her.)*

ABEL. Who is that goofy-lookin' old sot?

MELISSA. *(Returning* **HEPPENSTAHL**'s *wave.)* That's Mr. Heppenstahl, the pickle and mincemeat judge.

ABEL. Well, that explains it.

MELISSA. Explains what?

> *(For one horrible moment it looks as though they've both been caught in the mincemeat and brandy conspiracy.)*

ABEL. How about a dance with the prettiest girl at the fair?

MELISSA. Well I'd feel a little funny asking her, but you go right ahead.

ABEL. *(Pulling her into his arms.)* You know who I mean, Mother.

MELISSA. Why Abel Frake, you're so amorous.

ABEL.
MAYBE IT'S MORE THAN THE MOON.

MELISSA.
MAYBE IT'S MORE THAN THE BIRDS.

MELISSA & ABEL.
MAYBE IT'S MORE THAN THE SIGHT OF THE NIGHT
IN A LIGHT TOO LOVELY FOR WORDS.

> *(**EMILY** and **WAYNE** enter and join in the number.)*

WOMEN.
MAYBE IT'S MORE THAN THE EARTH.

MEN.
SHINY AND SILVERY BLUE.

ALL.
MAYBE THE REASON I'M FEELING THIS WAY
HAS SOMETHING TO DO WITH YOU.

IT'S A GRAND NIGHT FOR SINGING!
THE MOON IS FLYING HIGH,
AND SOMEWHERE A BIRD
WHO IS BOUND HE'LL BE HEARD
IS THROWING HIS HEART AT THE SKY,

IT'S A GRAND NIGHT FOR SINGING!
THE STARS ARE BRIGHT ABOVE,
THE EARTH IS AGLOW
AND TO ADD TO THE SHOW,
I THINK I AM FALLING IN LOVE –
FALLING, FALLING IN LOVE!

    (The music surges, and the stage is awhirl in a grand waltz; then:)

ABEL, CLAY, HANK & LEM. *(In barbershop harmony.)*
MAYBE IT'S MORE THAN THE MOON,
MAYBE IT'S MORE THAN THE BIRDS,
MAYBE IT'S MORE THAN THE SIGHT OF THE NIGHT
IN A LIGHT TOO LOVELY FOR WORDS.
MAYBE IT'S MORE THAN THE EARTH,
SHINY AND SILVERY BLUE.
MAYBE THE REASON I'M FEELING THIS WAY
HAS SOMETHING TO DO WITH YOU.

    (The waltz resumes; then:)

ALL. *(Beginning in a hushed staccato.)*
IT'S A GRAND NIGHT FOR SINGING!
THE MOON IS FLYING HIGH
AND SOMEWHERE A BIRD
WHO IS BOUND HE'LL BE HEARD,
IS THROWING HIS HEART AT THE SKY.
IT'S A GRAND NIGHT FOR SINGING!
THE STARS ARE BRIGHT ABOVE.
THE EARTH IS AGLOW
AND TO ADD TO THE SHOW,
I THINK I AM FALLING IN LOVE!
IT'S A GRAND NIGHT FOR SINGING!
THE STARS ARE BRIGHT ABOVE
THE EARTH IS AGLOW
AND TO ADD TO THE SHOW,
I THINK I AM FALLING IN LOVE –

ALL.

> FALLING...

>> *(***WAYNE** *and* **EMILY** *dance downstage, kiss passionately, and exit.)*

> FALLING...

>> *(***PAT** *and* **MARGY** *dance downstage, kiss passionately, and as they turn to exit,* **HARRY** *suddenly appears.)*

MARGY. Harry...?

HARRY. I bet you're surprised to see me!

MARGY. You have no idea.

>> *(***HARRY** *whisks her onto the dance floor as* **PAT** *looks on, bewildered.)*

ALL.

> FALLING...
> FALLING...
> IN LOVE!

>> *(The waltz continues exuberantly as the curtain slowly falls.)*

ACT II

[MUSIC NO. 16 "ENTR'ACTE"]

(The music segues directly into:)

[MUSIC NO. 16A "OPENING ACT II"]

Scene One
Outside the Livestock Pavilion
Friday Afternoon

(To one side of the stage is the entrance to the Livestock Pavilion upstage of the Information Booth. **FAIRGOERS** *are coming and going as* **MELISSA** *[wearing both her blue and red ribbons],* **MARGY, WAYNE,** *and* **HARRY** *enter.)*

FAIR ANNOUNCER. *(Offstage.)* Next up in the Livestock Pavilion – the Senior Class finalists for the Grand Sweepstakes.

MELISSA. That's Blue Boy!

WAYNE. We better get our seats.

> *(They hurry toward the entrance and are met head-on by* **ABEL,** *entering from the pavilion. He is fit to be tied. Music out.)*

ABEL. I have had all I can take! I am washing my hands of that rotten, ungrateful...

MELISSA. What is it, Abel?

WAYNE. What's wrong?

69

ABEL. That stinkin' boar has lost his mind, that's what! Here it is, his moment of glory, and he's back there layin' in the mud! There is just no getting him on his feet and out of that pen. I prodded, I pleaded, I sang him "Cow-Cow Boogie"! I am here to tell you – come Saturday supper, we're havin' one helluva pork roast!

MELISSA. *(Reassuringly.)* Now calm yourself, Abel. I have every confidence in Blue Boy.

(*To* **WAYNE**, *frantically.*) Wayne, you've got to do something fast!

WAYNE. C'mon, Harry – let's show that hog who's boss.

HARRY. You bet! If he wants to get tough, so can we!

> (**WAYNE** *and* **HARRY** *stalk off into the Livestock Pavilion.*)

ABEL. *(Following them offstage.)* Now you know how sensitive Blue Boy is! You harm one bristle on that boar's butt and I'll...

MARGY. Oh, Mama, this is terrible. What if Blue Boy loses?

MELISSA. We'll have to shoot him.

MARGY. Blue Boy?

MELISSA. No, your father.

> (*She races off into the pavilion, and* **MARGY** *follows.* **PAT,** *who has been sitting unnoticed to one side, reading the paper, calls to* **MARGY:**)

PAT. Whoa there, Bobbylocks – where's the fire?

MARGY. Oh, Pat, it's just terrible. This is Daddy's big event and Blue Boy's being temperamental. Wayne and Harry are back there with him right now. Harry's great with animals.

PAT. How is he with you?

MARGY. What...?

PAT. Are you in love with him?

MARGY. I...I guess I've known Harry forever. We went to kindergarten together and graduated high school together. People have always kinda paired us off. Harry and Margy, Margy and...

(She pauses.)

He wants to marry me.

PAT. What do you want?

MARGY. That's a funny question. I don't think anyone's ever asked me before.

PAT. Now that ya mention it, I don't think I've ever asked a girl that question.

MARGY. I guess you've had a lot of experience with girls.

PAT. I've done my share of running around, if that's what ya mean.

MARGY. But you've never been in love?

PAT. Oh sure – a hundred times.

(Beat.)

No, I haven't. Look, Bobbylocks, it's the last day of the fair so I'm gonna level with ya. I'm not the kinda guy I'd wish on a wonderful girl like you.

MARGY. So you're calling it quits.

PAT. No – I don't ever wanna call it quits with you!

(He moves to kiss her just as **ABEL** *enters from the pavilion.* **PAT** *discretely crosses away.)*

ABEL. How could he do this to me, after all we've meant to each other, after all we've been through together? Why would he deliberately wanna break my heart?

MARGY. I know how much winning the sweepstakes meant to you, Daddy.

ABEL. And I'd sooner plow the back forty with my face than lose that five-dollar bet to Dave Miller!

(**HANK** *enters from the pavilion.*)

HANK. Hiya, Abel.

ABEL. Well, if it isn't Hank Munson.

HANK. Well if it isn't, his wife didn't seem to mind! Say, isn't that Blue Boy's class they just called?

ABEL. It looks like Blue Boy won't be competin' after all.

HANK. Whaddaya talkin' about?

ABEL. He's had some kinda nervous collapse. He's layin' back there moanin' and wheezin'. It's...it's like he just lost his best friend.

HANK. Now that's peculiar. When I went back to get Esmerelda for her showing, he was struttin' around that pen proud as a peacock. Esmerelda and him were carryin' on quite a lively conversation.

[MUSIC NO. 16B "MUCH MORE THAN JUST A FRIEND (UNDERSCORE)"]

ABEL. Now hold on. You say Blue Boy was frisky enough when Esmerelda was in her pen right across from him, but when ya took her away...

HANK. Why of course, that's it!

(*A big glissando from the orchestra.*)

He's lovesick for my beauteous girl!

ABEL. C'mon, Hank!

(**ABEL** *and* **HANK** *hurry off into the pavilion. Music out.*)

PAT. *(Crossing to* **MARGY.***)* It looks like love really does conquer all.

MARGY. What could that stupid beast possibly know about love?

PAT. What do any of us know about love?

> *(***PAT*** takes* **MARGY***'s face in his hands and kisses her.)*

MARGY. I gotta get inside, Pat. Meet me tonight – outside the Dairy Pavilion at seven o'clock.

PAT. Anything you say.

> *(***MARGY*** hurries off into the Livestock Pavilion, leaving* **PAT** *alone to ponder the moment.)*

Anything you say? Well, would ya listen to me.

> *(***VIVIAN*** and* **JEANNE,** *the two cooch dancers, enter.)*

VIVIAN. Hey, Pat, we're throwin' a shower for Trudy tonight over at the Oasis. Trudy don't get off work till midnight but they're keepin' the dump open for us till dawn.

PAT. Thanks for the invite but I've sworn off.

JEANNE. Off what?

VIVIAN. And since when?

PAT. Off the high-life, starting now.

> *(***VIVIAN*** and* **JEANNE** *look to each other, disbelieving, then look back at* **PAT.***)*

[MUSIC NO. 17 "THE MAN I USED TO BE"]

VIVIAN.
YOU'VE CHANGED, BUB,
YOU'VE CHANGED A LOT.

JEANNE.

> AND THE GANG YOU USED TO GO WITH ALL CONCUR.
> YOU'VE CHANGED, BUB.

VIVIAN.

> YOU'RE NOT YOURSELF.

VIVIAN & JEANNE.

> IF THIS IS YOURSELF, YOU'RE NOT THE MAN YOU WERE!

> > (**PAT** *steps between them, takes their arms in a most gentlemanly manner, and crosses with them as he sings.*)

PAT.

> THE MAN I USED TO BE,
> A HAPPY MAN WAS HE,
> AND AIMLESS AS A LEAF IN A GALE.

VIVIAN & JEANNE.

> WHATEVER HAS BECOME
> OF THAT LIGHT-HEARTED BUM
> WHO THOUGHT HE HAD THE WORLD BY THE TAIL?

PAT.

> THE MAN I USED TO BE,
> HIS LIFE WAS GAY AND FREE
> AND AIMLESS AS A CLOUD IN THE SKY.
> HE THOUGHT HE KNEW THE GAME,
> THEN ALONG CAME A DAME
> WHO TURNED HIM INTO SOME OTHER GUY.
> I'VE GOT AMBITION NOW,
> I'VE GOT A MISSION NOW,
> I AIM TO REACH THE TOP OF THE TREE.
> THAT OTHER FLY-BY-NIGHT,
> WHO FLEW SO HIGH BY NIGHT,
> HAS VANISHED LIKE A SAIL ON THE SEA.
> AND I'LL NEVER FIND THAT EASY-LIVING,

EASY-TAKING, EASY-GIVING
FELLOW THAT I USED TO CALL ME.

ALL.

YOU CAN NEVER FIND THE MAN YOU USED TO BE.

PAT.

THE MAN I USED TO BE
WOULD GO TO SLEEP AT THREE
OR FOUR A.M.

JEANNE.

OR SEVEN.

VIVIAN.

OR NINE!

VIVIAN & JEANNE.

AND WHEN HIS WEARY HEAD
WASN'T NEAR ANY BED,
A TABLE OR A CHAIR WOULD BE FINE!

PAT.

A MAN WITHOUT A GOAL,
A SORT OF FRIENDLY SOUL,
HE LIKED TO PLAY THE ROLE OF A HOST
TO ANY THIRSTY PAL,

VIVIAN & JEANNE.

OR A CASUAL GAL
WHO'D STAY TO COOK HIS COFFEE AND TOAST.

ALL.

HE WAS A NE'ER-DO-WELL
WHO WOULDN'T DARE DO WELL,
HE NEVER SAW THE TOP OF A TREE.

PAT.

BUT KIND OF SAD I AM
TO SEE THE CAD I AM

ALL.

DISSOLVING LIKE A SAIL ON THE SEA.

PAT.

AND I'LL NEVER FIND THAT FATALISTIC,
FREE AND EASY, EGOTISTIC
OPTIMIST WHO USED TO BE ME.

ALL.

YOU CAN NEVER FIND THE MAN YOU USED TO BE.

(Music continues.)

JEANNE. Ya know, you used to be a real pistol, Gilbert.

VIVIAN. Looks like some skirt went and turned you into a
pop-gun.

*(**VIVIAN** and **JEANNE** share a hearty laugh as
they exit.)*

PAT. *(Tipping his hat.)* Have a lovely evening, ladies.

*(He dances with abandon, a carefree fellow in
the throes of first love, taking great pride in
the realization that he is indeed a new man.)*

YOU CAN NEVER FIND THE MAN YOU USED TO BE.

[MUSIC NO. 17A "INTO 'IOWAY'"]

*(A thundering ovation rises from the
Livestock Pavilion, and the **CROWD** comes
streaming onstage, chanting:)*

CROWD. *(Entering.)* Blue Boy! ...Blue Boy! ...Blue Boy! ...

*(**ABEL**, wearing his blue ribbon, is carried
aloft on the shoulders of **HANK** and **CLAY**.
A beaming **MELISSA** follows with **WAYNE**,
MARGY, and **HARRY**. **CHARLIE** is also in the
CROWD.)*

PAT. *(Crossing to* **ABEL.***)* Mr. Frake, how does it feel to own the most honored boar in the state?

ABEL. State, nothin'! Everybody knows, "Nothin' fine as Ioway swine!"

(The **CROWD** *cheers. Music out.)*

That makes Blue Boy the best boar in the universe!

(Again the **CROWD** *cheers as* **CHARLIE** *snaps a picture of* **ABEL.***)*

[MUSIC NO. 18 "ALL I OWE IOWAY"]

I CAN HEAR THEM CALLIN' HOGS
IN THE CLEAR IOWAY AIR.
I CAN SNIFF THE FRAGRANT WHIFF
OF AN IOWAY ROSE.

MELISSA.
YOU'VE GOT IOWAY IN YOUR HEART!

ABEL.
I'VE GOT IOWAY IN MY HAIR,
I'VE GOT IOWAY IN MY EARS
AND EYES AND NOSE!

OH, I KNOW
ALL I OWE
I OWE IOWAY.
I OWE IOWAY ALL I OWE AND I KNOW WHY.
I AM IOWAY BORN AND BRED
AND ON IOWAY CORN I'M FED,
NOT TO MENTION HER BARLEY, WHEAT AND RYE.

I OWE IOWAY FOR HER HAM
AND HER BEEF AND HER LAMB
AND HER STRAWBERRY JAM
AND HER PIE.

FIRST SOLOIST.
> I OWE IOWAY MORE THAN I CAN EVER PAY
> SO I THINK I'LL MOVE TO CALIFORN-I-AY!

ABEL, HANK, CLAY & LEM. *(In their usual barbershop harmony.)*
> WHAT A SHAME!
> WHAT A SHAME!
> YOU'LL BE GOOD AND GOSH-DARN SORRY WHEN YOU GO!

CROWD. Don't I know!

ABEL, HANK, CLAY & LEM.
> WHEN YOU LEAVE YOUR NATIVE STATE
> YOU'LL BE FEELIN' FAR FROM GREAT –
> YOU'LL BE GOOD AND GOSH-DARN SORRY WHEN YOU GO!

MELISSA.
> I'M A SEED OF IOWAY GRAIN.

WAYNE.
> YOU'RE A BREEZE THAT IOWAY BLEW.

HARRY.
> I'M A DROP OF IOWAY RAIN.

MARGY. *(To* **HARRY.***)*
> YOU'RE A DRIP...

> **(HARRY** *reacts, hurt.)*

> ...OF IOWAY DEW!

ALL. *(Variously.)*
> OH, I KNOW
> ALL I OWE
> I OWE IOWAY.
> I OWE IOWAY ALL I OWE AND I KNOW WHY.
> I AM IOWAY BORN AND BRED
> AND ON IOWAY CORN I'M FED,
> NOT TO MENTION HER BARLEY, WHEAT AND RYE.

ABEL.
>I OWE IOWAY FOR HER HAM,

MELISSA.
>AND HER BEEF AND HER LAMB,

MARGY.
>AND HER STRAWBERRY JAM,

WAYNE & HARRY.
>AND HER PIE!

SECOND SOLOIST.
>I OWE IOWAY MORE THAN ANYONE SHOULD OWE,
>SO I THINK I'LL START IN OWIN' IDAHO!

ABEL, HANK, CLAY & LEM.
>WHAT A SHAME!
>WHAT A SHAME!
>YOU'LL BE CRYIN' LIKE A BABY WHEN YOU GO!

CROWD. Don't I know!

ABEL, HANK, CLAY & LEM.
>WHEN YOU LEAVE YOUR NATIVE HEATH
>WITH YOUR LIP BETWEEN YOUR TEETH,
>YOU'LL BE BAWLIN' LIKE A BABY WHEN YOU GO!

ALL. *(Variously.)*
>OH, I KNOW
>ALL I OWE
>I OWE IOWAY.
>I OWE IOWAY ALL I OWE AND I KNOW WHY.
>I AM IOWAY BORN AND BRED
>AND ON IOWAY CORN I'M FED,
>NOT TO MENTION HER BARLEY, WHEAT AND RYE.
>I OWE IOWAY FOR HER HAM
>AND HER BEEF AND HER LAMB
>AND HER STRAWBERRY JAM
>AND HER PIE.

THIRD SOLOIST.

> THOUGH I'M OWIN' HER MORE THAN I CAN EVER PAY,
> IF SHE'LL KEEP ME ON THE CUFF, I'D LIKE TO STAY!

ABEL, HANK, CLAY & LEM. Now you're talkin'!

> BETTER STAY!
> BETTER STAY!
> YOU'LL BE GOOD AND GOSH-DARN HAPPY IF YOU DO!

ABEL & MELISSA.

> IF IOWAY IS YOUR HOME,
> YOU'RE A FOOL TO WANT TO ROAM
> 'CAUSE THERE CAN'T BE ANY BETTER HOME FOR YOU!

> > (**ABEL** *and* **MELISSA** *kick off a rollicking square dance, and soon the stage erupts with a rip-roarin', foot-stompin' country reel!*)

ALL. *(Chanting.)* Hey!

> Yay!
>
> I!
>
> O!
>
> W!
>
> A!
>
> Ioway!

> > *(Variously.)*

> OH, I KNOW
> ALL I OWE
> I OWE IOWAY.
> I OWE IOWAY ALL I OWE AND I KNOW WHY.
> I AM IOWAY BORN AND BRED
> AND ON IOWAY CORN I'M FED,
> NOT TO MENTION HER BARLEY, WHEAT AND RYE.
> I OWE IOWAY FOR HER HAM
> AND HER BEEF AND HER LAMB

AND HER STRAWBERRY JAM
AND HER PIE.

IF IOWAY IS YOUR HOME,
YOU'RE A FOOL TO WANT TO ROAM
'CAUSE THERE CAN'T BE ANY BETTER HOME FOR...

(Chanting in hushed excitement, building like a cheer:)

I-O-W...
I-O-W...
I-Q-I-O...
I-O-W-A!
'CAUSE THERE CAN'T BE ANY BETTER HOME FOR YOU!

Ioway!

[MUSIC NO. 18A "SCENE CHANGE"]

(The **CROWD** *exits as the scene shifts to reveal:)*

Scene Two
Outside the Dairy Pavilion
Early That Night

(**FAIRGOERS** *are strolling along as* **HARRY** *wanders across, looking for* **MARGY**. **PAT** *enters, dancing across the stage past* **HARRY** *as* **HARRY** *exits.*)

[MUSIC NO. 19 "THE MAN I USED TO BE (REPRISE)"]

PAT.

AND I'LL NEVER FIND THAT EASY-LIVING,
EASY-TALKING, EASY-GIVING
FELLOW THAT I USED TO CALL ME –
YOU CAN NEVER FIND THE MAN YOU USED TO BE...

(**CHARLIE** *enters urgently, interrupting* **PAT**'s *reverie.*)

CHARLIE. Hey, Gilbert – I been lookin' all over the grounds for ya.

PAT. So ya found me. What's up?

CHARLIE. Ya got a call from the Chicago Trib. Seems the managing editor has to fly to the coast so he's moved your interview up to first thing tomorrow. We got just enough time to get ya on the last train out tonight.

PAT. But I can't leave now. Margy's meeting me here.

CHARLIE. So you'll find another girl in Chicago.

PAT. She's not just another girl.

CHARLIE. And this is not just another job. This is the chance ya been waitin' for, Pat. Now if ya wanna throw it all away for some girl you've known for two days, it's no skin off my nose, but ya better decide fast 'cause that train's not gonna wait.

(He exits. PAT *takes a moment, looks at the bench.)*

PAT. Same old Pat.

(He races off after CHARLIE.*)*

[MUSIC NO. 20 "ISN'T IT KINDA FUN? (REPRISE)"]

(A few FAIRGOERS *are strolling along as* WAYNE *enters and crosses.* MARGY *enters and sees* WAYNE.*)*

MARGY. Meeting someone?

*(*WAYNE *spins around, caught off-guard.)*

WAYNE. Uh-huh.

*(*MARGY *sits down on the bench.)*

Waiting for someone?

MARGY. Uh-huh.

WAYNE. *(Crossing to her.)* I promise not to tell if you don't.

MARGY. *(Playfully holding up her little finger.)* Pinky swear?

*(*WAYNE *hooks his pinky with hers, then continues on his way.)*

WAYNE. *(Turning back.)* Want me to wait with ya?

MARGY. That's okay – you go ahead.

*(*WAYNE *starts off.)*

Wayne –

(He turns back to her.)

Thanks.

*(*WAYNE *exits.)*

MARGY.

> MAYBE WE'RE OUT FOR LAUGHS, A GIRL AND A BOY,
> KIDDING ACROSS A TABLE FOR TWO,
> BUT HAVEN'T YOU GOT A HUNCH THAT THIS IS THE REAL
>   MCCOY
> AND ALL THE THINGS WE TELL EACH OTHER...
> ARE TRUE?

> *(The music segues directly into:)*

> ### [MUSIC NO. 21 "THAT'S THE WAY IT HAPPENS"]

> *(A spotlight picks up **EMILY** at the microphone on the "stage" of the Starlight Dance Meadow. She wears a distinctly sexy gown.)*

EMILY.

> THAT'S THE WAY IT HAPPENS,
> THAT'S THE WAY IT HAPPENS...

> *(The music continues as the scene shifts to reveal:)*

Scene Three
The Starlight Dance Meadow
Immediately Following

EMCEE. *(Offstage.)* Before we bid a fond farewell to the Fair of '46, please welcome back Emily Arden and The Fairtones.

EMILY.
YOU'RE A GIRL FROM CHICAGO ON THE ROAD WITH A SHOW,
NOT A SOUL IN NEW HAVEN YOU CAN SAY YOU KNOW.
YOU WISH YOU WERE A MILE OR SO FROM MICHIGAN LAKE,
HOME WITH YOUR MOTHER AND A T-BONE STEAK.

> *(She is joined by* **THE FAIRTONES;** **WAYNE** *is revealed at a ringside table, enraptured by her performance.)*

THEN ALONG COMES A FELLOW WITH A SMILE LIKE A KID,
AND HE GETS YOUR ATTENTION WITH A TIMELY BID.
HE SAYS HE KNOWS A BISTRO WHERE THEY GIVE YOU A BREAK
WITH FRENCH-FRIED POTATOES AND A T-BONE STEAK.
THAT'S THE WAY IT HAPPENS.

THE FAIRTONES.
THAT'S THE WAY IT HAPPENS.

EMILY.
THAT'S THE WAY IT HAPPENS.

THE FAIRTONES.
THAT'S THE WAY IT HAPPENS.

EMILY.	**THE FAIRTONES.**
YOU ARE SHY AND UNCERTAIN, BUT HE PLEADS AND YOU YIELD,	DOOT DOOT DOOWAH DOOWAH

EMILY.	THE FAIRTONES.
AND YOU DON'T HAVE AN INKLING THAT YOU'RE SIGNED AND SEALED	DOWAH DOOT DOOT DOOWAH DOOWAH
BY MERELY TELLING SOMEONE YOU'D BE GLAD TO PARTAKE	DOOWAH DOOT DOOT DOOWAH DOOWAH
OF FRENCH-FRIED POTATOES AND A T-BONE STEAK.	DOOWAH DOOT DOOWAH
THAT'S THE WAY IT HAPPENS,	WAY IT HAPPENS.
THAT'S THE WAY IT HAPPENS.	WAY IT HAPPENS.
THAT'S THE WAY IT HAPPENED TO ME!	WAY IT IT HAPPENED TO ME!

(**EMILY** *and* **THE FAIRTONES** *go into a sultry jazz routine, by turns emotional and explosive.*)

THE FAIRTONES.
THAT'S THE WAY IT HAPPENS,
THAT'S THE WAY IT HAPPENS.

EMILY & THE FAIRTONES.
THAT'S THE WAY IT HAPPENED TO ME!

(*The* **CROWD** *applauds as* **EMILY** *and* **THE FAIRTONES** *take their bows.* **THE FAIRTONES** *exit.*)

[MUSIC NO. 21A "AFTER IT HAPPENS (UNDERSCORE)"]

(*A few* **COUPLES** *dance as* **WAYNE** *crosses from his table to meet* **EMILY.**)

WAYNE. Gee, you're a beautiful bundle of talent!

EMILY. Tell it to the Shuberts.

WAYNE. Tell it to 'em, nothin'! I'll put it on a billboard in Harold Square.

EMILY. Could you move it uptown to Times Square?

WAYNE. I'll put one there too!

(He takes her in his arms and they dance.)

So, how long until your next show?

EMILY. No late show tonight. The Miss Cora Silk Pageant takes over the hall.

WAYNE. So you're free?

EMILY. Fancy free. Until eleven-thirty.

WAYNE. Eleven-thirty...?

EMILY. Milwaukee, remember? My bus leaves at eleven-thirty.

WAYNE. Tonight? But it's the last night of the fair. I thought... I was hopin' we could spend it together.

EMILY. We can – until eleven-thirty. Give me a minute to change out of these glad rags.

(She exits. Music out. **VIOLET** *enters and races over to* **WAYNE.**)

VIOLET. Hey tiger!

WAYNE. Hey, Violet.

VIOLET. How 'bout a dance?

WAYNE. You're on, kid!

[MUSIC NO. 21B "VIOLET AND WAYNE'S JITTERBUG"]

*(***WAYNE*** *and* ***VIOLET*** *go into a rousing jitterbug, lifts and all.* ***WAYNE*** *sets* ***VIOLET*** *down and offers her his cheek. When she moves in to kiss him, he turns and plants a big one right on her kisser, then races off upstage.)*

VIOLET. *(Calling after him.)* I'll see *you* next year!

[MUSIC NO. 21C "SCENE CHANGE"]

*(*VIOLET *squeals with delight and runs off as* HARRY *wanders across, still looking for* MARGY, *and the scene shifts to reveal:)*

Scene Four
The Hillside
Later That Night

(EMILY sits on the raised clearing, WAYNE lying with his head in her lap. His sports jacket and her shoes lie next to the clearing. Music out.)

EMILY. You asleep?

WAYNE. No. Just dreamin'.

EMILY. About what?

WAYNE. Us. The past three days.

EMILY. Sounds like a nice dream.

(She moves to get up.)

It's getting late.

WAYNE. *(Stopping her.)* No – please. Just a little longer.

EMILY. We don't have a little longer.

(Putting on her shoes.) Greyhound waits for no man.

WAYNE. I'll walk ya to the station.

EMILY. No thanks. I think we better say goodbye right here.

WAYNE. *(Urgently.)* We can't say goodbye, Emily – not now. I know, I know – first rule of show business. But we weren't counting on falling in love. Can't we throw the rules away?

EMILY. No, Wayne, we can't. There's no way we…

WAYNE. Yes we can – we can try! I know we can work it out if we really *try*!

EMILY. I have tried, I'm married!

*(Her hand goes to her mouth as if to stop the words, but it's too late. **WAYNE** stares, not knowing whether or not to believe his ears.)*

EMILY. I haven't seen him in about a year. He got tired of sitting at home every time I went on the road. We spent the two and a half years of our marriage trying to arrange a weekend together. And the last time I left he said that if I walked out the door, he wouldn't be there when I got back. And you know what? I never got back. I won't let that happen again, especially with someone like you, Wayne. I don't like to see nice guys taken advantage of.

[MUSIC NO. 21D "UNDERSCORE / SCENE CHANGE"]

WAYNE. *(A pause; then, quietly.)* It might be different for ya this time. With me?

EMILY. Trust me, Wayne, I know what I'm good at. I'll never make a great wife – I might make a great entertainer.

*(**WAYNE** grabs his jacket and crosses to exit.)*

Can you look at it this way?

(He stops, his back to her.)

Three days ago you came to the fair and you didn't even know a girl named Emily. Then we met, and we ended up taking a trip to the moon, and then we came back to Earth. So does that put you ahead or behind?

*(**WAYNE** exits, not looking back, leaving **EMILY** alone.)*

(To herself.) Always leave 'em laughing.

(She exits as the scene shifts to reveal:)

Scene Five
Camper's Hill
Later That Night

(**ABEL** *and* **MELISSA** *are sitting on the picnic bench, enjoying each other's company. Music out.*)

MELISSA. It's so quiet... Such a beautiful summer sky.

ABEL. That North Star's the one'll be leadin' us home tomorrow.

MELISSA. Which one?

ABEL. You don't know that?

MELISSA. Tell me again.

(**ABEL** *pulls her close with his arm around her shoulder, pointing out the stars.*)

ABEL. See the Big Dipper? Take those last two stars in the bowl and right beyond them, a little to the left, that's the north star. My grandfather set his fences on that star.

MELISSA. A night like this makes me feel like we're the only two people in the world.

ABEL. And we're sittin' right here on top of it. I can't wait to see the look on Dave Miller's face tomorrow after supper – both of us victorious, Margy and Wayne havin' the time of their lives!

MELISSA. I haven't seen Margy and Wayne since supper.

ABEL. Oh calm yourself, Mother – it's the last night o' the fair. Ya know, we're gonna have to start givin' some thought to lettin' loose o' the reins on those two.

MELISSA. I'm worried about Margy. She promised Harry an answer after the fair and I'm afraid it might not be the one he's been counting on. Then what?

ABEL. Then she'll, marry somebody else.

[MUSIC NO. 22 "BOYS AND GIRLS LIKE YOU AND ME"]

Why sure, one day Margy'll come running home all in a tizzy over some new fella she met and ain't he the cat's butt. I mean, isn't that what always happens?

THEY WALK ON EVERY VILLAGE STREET,
THEY WALK IN LANES WHERE BRANCHES MEET,
AND STARS SEND DOWN THEIR BLESSINGS FROM THE
  BLUE.
THEY GO THROUGH STORMS OF DOUBT AND FEAR,
AND SO THEY GO FROM YEAR TO YEAR,
BELIEVING IN EACH OTHER AS WE DO,
BRAVELY MARCHING FORWARD TWO BY TWO.

BOYS AND GIRLS LIKE YOU AND ME
WALK BENEATH THE SKIES.
THEY LOVE JUST AS WE LOVE,
WITH THE SAME DREAM IN THEIR EYES.
SONGS AND KINGS AND MANY THINGS
HAVE THEIR DAY AND ARE GONE,
BUT BOYS AND GIRLS LIKE YOU AND ME,
WE GO ON AND ON.

(The music continues.)

MELISSA. Well here it is, the moment every mother dreads. The children have grown up and somehow I didn't notice. I'm just so used to treatin' 'em like my babies, and it's such a hard habit to break.

ABEL. That it is. But just think, Mother – pretty soon we'll be right back where we started. I'll have you all to myself again.

BOYS AND GIRLS LIKE YOU AND ME
WALK BENEATH THE SKIES.

MELISSA.
> THEY LOVE JUST AS WE LOVE,
> WITH THE SAME DREAM IN THEIR EYES.

MELISSA & ABEL.
> SONGS AND KINGS
> AND MANY THINGS
> HAVE THEIR DAY AND ARE GONE,
> BUT BOYS AND GIRLS LIKE YOU AND ME,
> WE GO ON AND ON,
> WE GO ON AND ON.

> *(They kiss.* **HARRY** *enters.)*

ABEL. Hiya, Harry.

HARRY. Margy back yet?

MELISSA. She and Wayne must still be on the midway.

HARRY. It's gettin' pretty late. I think the fair's over.

> *(Crossing.)* Well, I guess I'll take a stroll down the other way. If she gets back, would ya tell her I need to talk to her?

MELISSA. Of course.

> *(**HARRY** starts to exit.)*

Harry, would you like some company? I'll walk you partway.

> *(**MELISSA** takes his arm and they exit, leaving the forsaken **ABEL** shrugging his shoulders at being abandoned by his sweetheart. **WAYNE** stumbles on, carrying a pint bottle of liquor and looking a mess.)*

ABEL. *(To himself, sensing that something has gone wrong.)* Uh-oh – Waldo Emerson.

WAYNE. *(Accusingly, slurring his speech in spite of valiant efforts not to.)* I suppose ya think I been drinking.

ABEL. Not till ya mentioned it.

WAYNE. Well...I had to. I'm drinking to forget.

ABEL. Is it working?

WAYNE. No.

ABEL. Never does.

WAYNE. I'll never forget Eleanor...I mean Emily.

ABEL. Oops. Little slip o' the tongue?

WAYNE. Oh, no...how could I be so stupid? I think I made an ass o' myself.

ABEL. *(Taking the bottle from* **WAYNE.***)* Men have been makin' fools o' themselves over women ever since Adam and Eve. I don't expect that's gonna change any time soon.

　　　　(He takes a swing from the bottle.)

So this Emily gal treated ya pretty rough, huh?

WAYNE. Yes! She made me feel... No. We had a wonderful time – a ride to the moon.

ABEL. Well, son, when ya fly that high, it most often ends with a bumpy landing.

WAYNE. I don't feel so good.

ABEL. You don't look so good. What say we walk it off and talk it over?

　　　　(Helping **WAYNE** *to his feet.)* C'mon, now – put your arm around your old man's shoulder – that's it.

WAYNE. Pop, do ya think Eleanor will ever forgive me?

ABEL. It might not be best to bother Eleanor with all the particulars. Sometimes it's more important to forgive yourself.

[MUSIC NO. 23 "SCENE CHANGE"]

(**WAYNE** *ponders what his father has said as they exit and the scene shifts to reveal:)*

Scene Six
On the Midway
Immediately Following

(The lights of the fair have gone out, the rides have been dismantled; a stack of packing crates are piled to one side. The CHIEF OF POLICE *strolls past* TWO ROUSTABOUTS *who are folding a banner that reads, "Welcome to the 1946 Iowa State Fair."* EMILY *crosses upstage with her suitcase and exits as* MARGY *enters despondently.)*

CHIEF OF POLICE. *(To* MARGY.*)* Say, little lady, it's awful late to be out here all by your lonesome.

MARGY. I was meeting someone. I guess he got held up.

FIRST ROUSTABOUT. Yeah – held up and tied down. She's been sitting over by the Dairy Pavilion all night.

CHIEF OF POLICE. Well, you get home safe now.

MARGY. I will. Thank you.

(The CHIEF OF POLICE *exits as the* ROUSTABOUTS *pack the banner into a crate.)*

SECOND ROUSTABOUT. Well, that about does it.

FIRST ROUSTABOUT. Yep. Next stop – 1947.

(They exit.)

MARGY. Well, Pat, it's not like you didn't warn me. You said any time you wanted to call it quits, you just wouldn't be around.

I LEAPT BEFORE I LOOKED
AND I GOT HOOKED.
I PLAYED WITH FIRE AND BURNED –
THAT'S HOW I LEARNED.

I MUST ADMIT I OWE A LOT TO YOU –
FROM NOW ON I WILL KNOW WHAT NOT TO DO.

THE NEXT TIME IT HAPPENS
I'LL BE WISE ENOUGH TO KNOW
NOT TO TRUST MY EYESIGHT
WHEN MY EYES BEGIN TO GLOW.

THE NEXT TIME I'M IN LOVE
WITH ANYONE LIKE YOU,
MY HEART WILL SING NO LOVE SONG
TILL I KNOW THE WORDS ARE TRUE,

"THE NEXT TIME IT HAPPENS" –
WHAT A FOOLISH THING TO SAY!
WHO EXPECTS A MIRACLE
TO HAPPEN EV'RY DAY?
IT ISN'T IN THE CARDS
AS FAR AS I CAN SEE
THAT A THING SO BEAUTIFUL AND WONDERFUL
COULD HAPPEN MORE THAN ONCE TO ME.

THE NEXT TIME I'M IN LOVE
WITH ANYONE LIKE YOU,
MY HEART WILL SING NO LOVE SONG
TILL I KNOW THE WORDS ARE TRUE.

"THE NEXT TIME IT HAPPENS" –
WHAT A FOOLISH THING TO SAY!
WHO EXPECTS A MIRACLE
TO HAPPEN EV'RY DAY?
IT ISN'T IN THE CARDS
AS FAR AS I CAN SEE
THAT A THING SO BEAUTIFUL AND WONDERFUL
COULD HAPPEN MORE THAN ONCE...
COULD HAPPEN MORE THAN ONCE...
COULD HAPPEN MORE THAN ONCE TO ME!

(**MARGY** *crosses to exit.*)

HARRY. *(Offstage.)* Margy...

(**MARGY** *turns expectantly as* **HARRY** *enters.*)

MARGY. Oh, Harry...it's you.

HARRY. Where've ya been, Marge?

MARGY. Watching 'em take down the fair. It's so magical when ya first see it – all lit up and in motion. Then it all comes apart and it's nothing like ya thought it was.

HARRY. Nope, it's all just canvas and plywood.

MARGY. Harry, I promised you an answer after the fair.

[MUSIC NO. 23A "GOODBYE, HARRY (UNDERSCORE)"]

I know how much you care about me, and I care about you, too – I really do. But I can't marry you. I'm sorry, Harry, sorrier than you can imagine. You're a terrific guy...

HARRY. If I'm so terrific then why won't you marry me? Just tell me what ya want – tell me what to do and I'll do it.

MARGY. There's nothing you can do.

HARRY. What have I done wrong?

MARGY. You haven't done anything wrong.

HARRY. Then is there somebody else?

MARGY. No.

HARRY. Then marry me!

MARGY. I can't! Don't ya see, Harry? I'm not in love with you.

(**HARRY** *lets this sink in for a moment.*)

HARRY. I guess somehow I always knew that, but I thought if I stuck around long enough, maybe you'd grow to love me. I guess I'm the kinda guy who needs to be hit in the head with a frying pan before he gets the message, but I've got it now – loud and clear. And here's some news for you, Miss Margy Frake. There'll come a day when you'll be good and sorry ya let me get away. I woulda given you everything.

> *(He exits, leaving* **MARGY** *visibly moved. Music out.)*

MARGY. *(To herself.)* Goodbye, Harry.

[MUSIC NO. 23B "SCENE CHANGE"]

> *(***MARGY*** *exits slowly as the scene shifts to reveal:)*

Scene Seven
The Frake Farm
Saturday Night After Supper

> (**ABEL** *is on the porch, reading the newspaper.*
> *He turns the page and something catches his*
> *eye. Music out.*)

ABEL. Well, I'll be breaded and deep-fried!

> (*Shouting.*) Mother, get out here – we're famous!

MELISSA. (*Entering in the kitchen, carrying supper dishes.*)
Why does he do this to me? He knows I can't hear him
from the dining room.

> (*She puts the dishes on the counter and*
> *crosses out the screen door.*)

What on earth are you hollerin' about out here?

ABEL. (*Holding the paper up for her to see.*) Get a load of
this!

MELISSA. (*Reading.*) "Iowa Pride – One Prizewinning
Family..." My stars, it's us!

ABEL. There's that picture of you winnin' the plaque!

MELISSA. And a picture of the fellas carryin' you out after
Blue Boy won!

ABEL. And look – a picture of Margy.

MELISSA. That newspaper fella really got around.

ABEL. You said a mouthful. Listen to this –

[MUSIC NO. 23C "PROUD IOWAY (UNDERSCORE)"]

> (*He reads from the paper:*)

"But it was their youngest, Miss Margaret Elizabeth
Frake, who guided me into the heart of her family.

(As **ABEL** *continues,* **MARGY** *enters in the kitchen, carrying supper dishes.)*

Whether clutching her mother's arm in support of her mincemeat or consoling her father when things looked darkest for his Hampshire boar, Margy represents what remains remarkable about the American family – win, place or show, they were all in it together."

(Music out.)

MELISSA. Margy, come see! We're in the newspaper!

*(***MARGY*** crosses out to* **MELISSA** *and* **ABEL.***)*

ABEL. Look – a big article by that Gilbert fella, and a picture of you.

MARGY. *(Studying the paper.)* When did he...

(Crossing away.) I don't know why he'd put a stupid picture of me in the paper, I didn't win anything.

ABEL. You little dickens – you knew this article was in the pipeline all along!

MARGY. I didn't know. Honest I didn't.

[MUSIC NO. 23D "ISN'T IT KINDA SAD? (UNDERSCORE)"]

You see, Mr. Gilbert approached me the first day of the fair and asked if...well, if he could spend some time with me, but he didn't tell me it was to...

(It all starts making sense to her as she crosses away, spinning out this scenario.)

Why, of course. He just wanted to write about one family's experience at the fair without them knowin'. So he used me. I guess it turned into something more than I thought it would.

ABEL. I'll say – it's spread over two whole pages! Wait'll Dave Miller catches wind of this – he's gonna spit sixpenny nails!

(We hear the honk of the familiar horn that signals DAVE MILLER's arrival. Music out.)

MELISSA. Speak of the devil.

ABEL. He better have a fiver on him he's ready to part company with.

(MILLER enters, carrying a stack of newspapers.)

Hiya, Dave. What's the good *news*?

MILLER. I kinda figured you'd wanna rub my nose in it.

(He hands the papers to ABEL.)

ABEL. That's mighty thoughtful of ya, Dave.

MELISSA. *(Taking the papers from ABEL.)* You're just in time for some cake and coffee, Mr. Miller.

MILLER. Thank you, Mrs. Frake, don't mind if I do.

MELISSA. Margy, come give me a hand.

(MELISSA and MARGY cross into the kitchen.)

ABEL. I'm surprised ya got room in your belly for cake 'cause I know ya been eatin' crow!

MILLER. Mark my words, Abel – it's bad enough you and the Mrs. both takin' top honors, but this newspaper story? If I was you, I'd keep my eyes peeled for an act of God.

ABEL. Yeah, well I won the bet in spite o' all your hocus-pocus. Now cough up that fin, ya old skinflint!

MILLER. Not so fast. Somethin' mighta happened we don't know about yet.

(WAYNE and ELEANOR enter excitedly upstage.)

Hello there, Wayne.

(Disappointed by WAYNE's obvious happiness.) I guess you musta had a dandy time at the fair – you sure do seem happy.

WAYNE. Happiest man alive –

(To ELEANOR.) – and the luckiest, too.

(Calling into the house.) Hey Mom, Margy – c'mon out here for a minute.

ELEANOR. *(Taking WAYNE's arm as MELISSA and MARGY cross out onto the porch.)* Go ahead, honeybunch – you tell 'em.

WAYNE. Well, we decided that next summer, when Eleanor gets home from college –

> *(Everyone leans in with eager anticipation, suspecting what the announcement will be.)*

We're gonna get engaged!

MILLER. From bad to worse!

MELISSA. Well...I hardly know what to say. What does that make you now?

ABEL. *(Very encouraging.)* Why, they're engaged to be engaged! Isn't this good news!

(Shaking WAYNE's hand.) Congratulations, son!

WAYNE. Thanks, Pop.

ELEANOR. C'mon, honeybunch – let's go tell *my* folks!

> *(They exit as ABEL crosses to MILLER, his hand open for the five dollars.)*

MILLER. We haven't heard from Margy yet.

MILLER. *(Crossing toward* **MARGY.***)* Hello, Margy. Did you have a good time at the fair?

>*(**MELISSA** and **ABEL** look to **MARGY** expectantly.)*

MARGY. Well...

>*(She looks from* **ABEL** *to* **MELISSA***, not knowing how to respond.)*

Let's just say that maybe I've outgrown the fair, Mr. Miller.

>*(She turns away.)*

MILLER. *(With a gleeful look to* **ABEL.***)* What a shame.

[MUSIC NO. 24 "FINALE ULTIMO"]

>*(**GUS** leads **PAT** on downstage, then exits.)*

Something downright tragic musta happened to make ya feel that way.

PAT. Hiya, Margy.

MARGY. *(Spinning around.)* Pat...?

PAT. Sorry I'm late.

MARGY. *(Crossing to him.)* Why didn't you meet me? I waited alone all night on that bench! Now you show up and expect me to just...

>*(She falls into his arms, and they kiss as the music swells.)*

PAT. I got a job, Margy. A real, job on a real paper – the Chicago Tribune. I wanna take you for a ride on that roller coaster.

>*(He looks from* **ABEL** *to* **MELISSA***, then gets down on one knee.)*

Margy...

MARGY. Yes, Pat – yes!

> *(Again they kiss as* **ABEL** *crosses to* **MILLER**. *No longer able to delay the inevitable,* **MILLER** *takes out a five-dollar bill and slaps it into* **ABEL***'s waiting palm.* **MELISSA** *allows* **ABEL** *a moment of glory before taking the bill from him and putting it away in her bosom for safekeeping, as the curtain falls.)*

The End

[MUSIC NO. 25 "BOWS"]

THE COMPANY.
OUR STATE FAIR IS A GREAT STATE FAIR –
DON'T MISS IT, DON'T EVEN BE LATE.
IT'S DOLLARS TO DOUGHNUTS THAT OUR STATE FAIR
IS THE BEST STATE FAIR IN OUR STATE!

[MUSIC NO. 26 "EXIT MUSIC"]

Milton Keynes UK
Ingram Content Group UK Ltd.
UKHW021833291123
433504UK00013B/644